Faith and Brooks were close,

♥ ♥ ♥

her arms around his neck and his around her waist. They were swaying just a little, every once in a while taking a tiny step. Brooks's curls were soft against the side of her face, and her long hair flowed over his shoulder. She could almost feel the soothing beat of his heart. She dropped one of her hands and slid it under his sweater, touching his smooth, bare back.

Then they were kissing. Short kisses first, leading to longer ones that made Faith nearly dizzy—nearly happy.

Yet Faith was aware that something was missing. Her heart didn't seem connected to her lips or arms.

♥ ♥ ♥

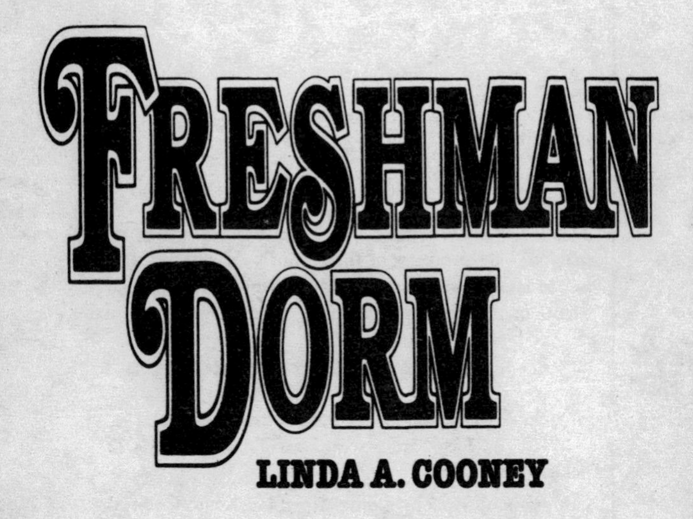

LINDA A. COONEY

HarperPaperbacks
A Division of HarperCollins*Publishers*

This is a work of fiction. The characters, incidents, and dialogues are products of the author's imagination and are not to be construed as real. And resemblance to actual events or persons, living or dead, is entirely coincidental.

HarperPaperbacks *A Division of* HarperCollins*Publishers*
10 East 53rd Street, New York, N.Y. 10022

Cover art by Tony Greco

First printing: September, 1990

Printed in the United States of America

HarperPaperbacks and colophon are trademarks of HarperCollins*Publishers*

10 9 8 7 6 5 4

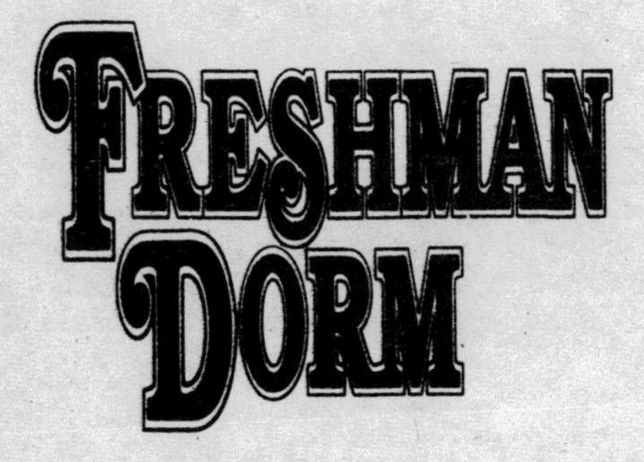
FRESHMAN
DORM

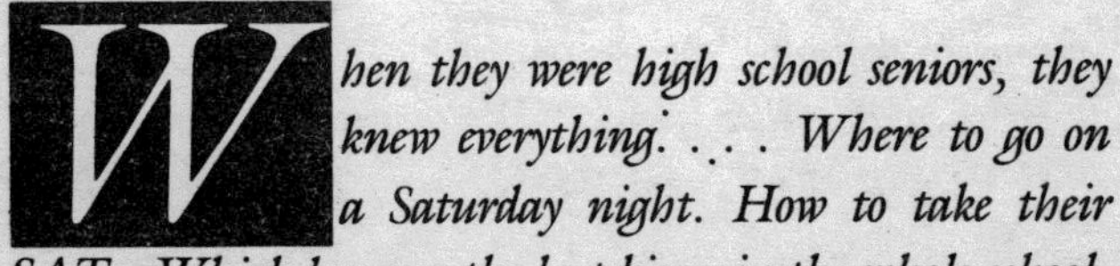

When they were high school seniors, they knew everything. . . . Where to go on a Saturday night. How to take their SATs. Which boy was the best kisser in the whole school.

By April they were ready to think about the future.

It was the Friday before spring break, and the three of them had skipped seventh period to sneak up to Lassen Lake. Actually, Winnie had cut the whole day, but KC had waited until she finished her economics quiz and Faith had called home first to make sure it was all right.

"Okay, Win, are you going to tell us why this get-together is so important?" Faith asked after they'd hiked down past the picnic tables and sat together on the small

pier. Snow still rimmed the mountains, but a trout jumped, leaving a bright ring on the water.

"Let me guess," KC answered instead. She sat stiffly on the wooden planks, trying not to get dirty. "You've decided that it's selfish to spend this coming summer in Europe alone, so you've arranged for Faith and me to come along."

"Don't I wish!" Winnie laughed, dangling her purple plastic sandals over the lake. "Faith wouldn't want to be away from Brooks for a whole summer, and KC, you'd probably want to visit every single stock exchange. So I guess I'll have to go alone." She sighed. "I'll miss you guys, though."

Faith touched her arm. "We'll miss you, too."

"We will," KC said. "Nothing's the same without you."

"At least we're going to college together," said Faith. "It's not like we'll be apart forever."

"I know. Hey, I got my dorm application from Springfield. Did you get yours?" Winnie asked.

Faith nodded.

"Mine came last week," KC said.

"Well?" Winnie stared and waited. "That's what we have to talk about! What are we going to write on our applications? Which dorm are we going to pick?"

"Winnie," Faith objected, "can't we do this after vacation?"

"Seize the moment. I, for one, don't believe in putting things off."

"Except homework," cracked KC.

"Really." Winnie giggled. As she threw her head back her four earrings and satin baseball jacket glimmered in the sun. "Besides, if I don't fill that application out as soon as I get home, I'll probably forget."

"It's easy," Faith decided. "We should just get a triple and room together."

"Are you sure?" KC was staring off at the water. "Maybe we don't all want to live in the same kind of dorm."

Faith let out a little gasp.

"Think about it," KC prodded. "What do we want in our college dorms? We haven't really talked about it."

"I guess we should tell each other," Winnie suggested.

"We should. Have we been best friends since eighth grade or haven't we?"

"We have, Faith," Winnie sighed. "We have."

Still, they sat silently as the water lapped and birds circled overhead. No one wanted to go first.

"All right," KC said. "I'll start with Winnie's ideal dorm."

"Mine?"

"Yours." KC sat up straighter and grinned. "First of all, there are no rules. There's a party every day.

Stereos are blasting all the time. And it's definitely coed—all guys except for Winnie!"

"Oh, yes!" Winnie howled and pounded the pier. She looked at Faith. "Faith's ideal dorm is full of drama types. But not weird drama types—nice drama types. And it's right next to Brooks's dorm, so she and Brooks can lean out their windows every night and pledge their love for all eternity."

KC and Winnie made corny kiss-kiss *noises and hummed lovey-dovey music. Faith put her hands over her face and shrieked.*

"Okay, okay!" Faith lifted her face. "In KC's ideal dorm there are special hours where everyone has to concentrate on getting ahead. You have to choose your future corporation by Thanksgiving break and do something productive every day just to get in the front door."

"That's right!" KC pumped her fist in the air.

The three of them started laughing, nudging each other, and flicking drops of cold, clear water. But gradually their mood turned more serious.

"We'll never agree on a dorm if we really want to live together, will we?" Winnie admitted.

"I don't think so," said Faith.

"So what do we do?"

KC held up her hands. "Each of us should go ahead and decide on her own dorm. If we pick the same one, we'll live together. . . ."

"And if we don't?" Faith gulped.

Winnie sighed. "We'll live apart."

Another silence followed. KC hummed to herself. Faith looked longingly back at the shore. Winnie fidgeted.

Finally Faith stated in a strong, clear voice, "No matter what dorm we live in, we'll always be friends."

"Of course," KC reassured her. "There's no question about that."

Winnie began to smile again. She tossed her head and her earrings jingled. "It'll take a lot more than living in a different dorm for you two to get rid of me."

"I've been waiting for college since tenth grade," KC said. "I know it's going to be great."

"It will be great," Faith agreed. "Brooks will be there. And so will both of you."

Suddenly KC shot up and hollered to the sky, "I'm so glad we're finally getting out of high school!"

Winnie jumped up next to her and yelled, "Freedom!"

Faith joined them and burst out laughing. "Justice!"

"And liberty for all dorms!" *they cried at the same time.*

Then they laughed and came together for a long, fierce hug.

One

aith made it there first.

She, Brooks, and her family stood at the edge of the south parking lot, near her dorm. She couldn't wait to throw herself into college life as a University of Springfield freshman. Yet there was something nagging at her.

Faith didn't want to cut off anything beloved from her past. She looked at her father and got a little bit worried and scared. Would she be able to get along without him now that she was going to be on her own?

"I'm so happy for you, Faith. This is going to be such an exciting time for you," Faith's father was saying, his gruff voice breaking with emotion.

"I'm glad Winnie, KC, and Brooks will be here with you, too."

Brooks tucked his arm around Faith's slim waist. "I'll look after her, Dr. Crowley. I always do."

Faith held back tears. "Oh, Brooks, I don't need looking after. I can look after myself," she told him, even though she wasn't quite sure herself.

Dr. Crowley cleared his throat. Then all of them—Faith, her mom, her sixteen-year-old sister, Marlee, her dad, and Brooks—were painfully quiet. They stared off at the clumps of dormitories, the other freshmen scurrying by, the scrubby brown mountains beyond. A ferocious volleyball game was being played on the dorm green. A horn honked. Wind rattled tall trees and the sun beat down. No one wanted to really say goodbye.

Finally Faith's mom broke the silence. "We can't forget Faith's presents," she said.

"Right. Of course. Thanks for reminding me." Dr. Crowley reached into the front seat of his Jeep, past his veterinarian's bag. A second later, two lumpy packages appeared. He thrust the parcels into Faith's arms.

"What are they?"

"Something old and something new." Her mom smiled, winking at Marlee. "It was Marlee's idea."

"I didn't mean it like you were getting married," Marlee blurted. "They're starting-college presents."

"I know." Faith kissed Brooks's cheek and gave him one package to hold. He laughed and then they were all staring at Faith again.

"Oh. Sorry." Faith tore into the paper. "I guess I'm supposed to open them."

"Duh." Marlee rolled her eyes. "I guess so."

Faith tore into one of the packages. As soon as she had shredded one corner of the paper, she knew what it was.

"My old bear!" Faith gasped, hugging the bear to her chest. It wore suspenders and a felt hat, and Faith had dragged it with her everywhere when she was a kid.

"I know it's silly," her mother said. "But Marlee and I thought you might like to have it in your dorm room."

"Sort of as a joke," added Marlee.

Faith threw her arms around her mother. "I love it." She hugged the bear again, but felt self-conscious as she noticed other freshman rushing by with their racing skis, computers, and high-tech stereos.

"And now for the something new," her father announced proudly. He gestured to Brooks, who presented the second package.

Faith handed the bear to Marlee, then ripped at paper again.

"Oh, Brooks, look! It's a book bag!"

"Look inside, honey."

Faith glanced up at her father, who nodded. She undid the buckles and opened up the bag.

When she saw what had been packed inside, she felt a clutch in her throat and then tears were slipping down her face. There was a clipboard, a flashlight pen, a stopwatch, a ruler, a compass, and a *Theatercrafts* magazine. "How did you know I needed all this?"

"I asked your old drama teacher what a drama major should have," her father confessed.

"Oh, Dad." Faith threw her arms around her father. At Lewis and Clark, her small-town high school, she'd been in the drama club and had worked backstage. She'd even directed a scene from *The Taming of the Shrew* that had won first place at the Western High-School Drama Festival.

Then they were all quiet again. Brooks picked up the discarded paper and tape. Faith's father jangled his car keys. Her mother watched while Marlee handed the bear back to Faith. There was no putting it off any longer: it was time to say goodbye.

"Honey, I have to see that mare at the Walker farm before dark," her father finally said.

"I know." Faith hugged him one last time. She

kissed her mother while her dad shook Brooks's hand.

"We love you, honey. We're so proud of you," her mom whispered.

Faith turned to Marlee. "Bye, nutcase." She had planned to smile, but when she held Marlee a fresh burst of tears exploded down her cheeks.

Marlee held on fiercely. "I'll miss you so much."

"I'll miss you, too," Faith cried. "But you'll be fine. Just like I'll be fine. Better than fine." She separated from her sister and took a few steps back. "Don't drive Mom and Dad too crazy."

Slowly, Faith's parents and sister piled into the Jeep.

Faith covered her eyes. "I can't stand it. Just go already. *Go!*"

"Bye," Marlee called.

"We love you, Faith."

"I love you. See you at Thanksgiving."

"Take care of her, Brooks!"

"I will." Then the engine roared and pieces of gravel crunched under the Jeep's fat tires. Faith's mom tried to scrub away the tears wetting her face, and her dad tried to smile. Marlee pressed her face against the back window and raised her hand. The Jeep was moving faster, rolling, circling and pulling away from the jumble of cars and lawns and bicycle racks.

Finally they were gone. Faith stood frozen, long after they'd disappeared. "They're gone," she whispered.

"It's about time." Brooks smiled and faced her, weaving his arms around her back. His bright eyes and loose blond curls gleamed in the afternoon sun. He moved closer, touching his nose to hers. "And we're here."

"We are, aren't we? We're really here."

Faith let herself have one last moment of longing for her family, then engulfed Brooks with her arms, taking in his optimism, his familiar sturdiness and dependable warmth. At least she hadn't had to leave him behind. Brooks would be the connection between her old life and her new one, a link between their small town of Jacksonville and U of S, a state university with almost twenty thousand students. Brooks would be her bridge—along with KC and Winnie, of course.

Brooks held her shoulders, kissed her, and smiled his winning, sure, senior-class-president smile. "You ready to move in and meet your roommate?"

She gulped. "Ready as I'll ever be."

He took Faith's new book bag and slung it over his shoulder. They began to walk away from the parking lot toward the dorm green, where students sunbathed, flipped Frisbees, and crossed back and forth, loaded down with duffels and books.

"Do you know where to meet Winnie and KC?"

"They're supposed to find me."

"Okay." Brooks climbed up and over a bench, stopping just at the edge of the grass. "Then are you ready to race me across the green?"

Faith acted coy, looking down at her feet and sticking her hands in her pockets. "Nah."

"Okay." Brooks gave a shrug and began to walk.

And that's when Faith took off, her gold braid slapping against her back, her feet exploding in her cowboy boots. "Come on, slowpoke," she yelled back. "Hurry up. There's no turning back now!"

Winnie and KC had made it to The Beanery, a coffee house just off campus. Sitting at a heavy wooden table, they were shuffling their feet on the sawdust-covered floor, soaking up the folky atmosphere and gulping frothy cappuccino.

"KC, you are amazing."

"Me?"

"You."

"Why, Win?"

"We ride two hours stuffed into your father's van. I feel like a grunged-out sardine, and you just walk into one of the hippest off-campus U of S hangouts and nail a part-time job."

"I need a job."

"If it were me, we'd still be kneeling at the feet of the manager of the Springfield Taco Bell."

KC laughed. "You just need to present yourself with confidence, Winnie. You have to know who to talk to and what to say," KC explained. She was wearing an understated blouse and a long, straight skirt. Elegant and tall, KC always seemed to know what to say. That combined with purposeful gray eyes and spectacular dark, wavy hair, made KC seem persuasive.

"Well, I'm just glad to finally be here." Winnie grinned. She looked artsy in baggy black trousers, black topped duck shoes, a man's vest, and a black beret. She and KC sipped hot coffee, munched cookies, and glanced around at the folk singer and the guys.

"I can't wait to meet my roommate," Winnie stated. "I sent her postcards from Europe. 'I'm in love. Having a great time, wish you were here. I'm in love again.' Come to think of it, she never wrote back."

"I envy you, Win."

"You could have had a roommate. I don't know how anyone could stand to live alone." Winnie flopped over the table and tapped KC's watch. When they'd ordered their coffees, KC had put it on the table between them as a reminder not to waste too much time.

"I *want* to live alone," KC protested.

Winnie laughed. "And you will, in that twenty-four-hour-quiet dorm. Someone told me they call it the morgue."

"Well, I don't envy you, living in some wild party dorm where you can't study and you can barely sleep. What I do envy is your whole summer away. I've been dying to be out on my own since I was about fifteen!" KC sat up taller. "Maybe I should have run away."

"Right," Winnie cracked. "I can just see you packing up your briefcase. Where would you have gone?"

"To your house."

"Really. Or Faith's," Winnie giggled.

KC shoved the cookies away, then began breaking off little pieces and popping them in her mouth. "What I mean, Win, is that you have this terrific advantage now because of what you've seen on your trip."

Winnie let a moment of sadness show, then put on a Groucho Marx voice and pretended to flick a cigar. "And this summer, KC, I saw plenty. It was *très* wild. I haven't told you all of it yet."

"Winnie, I'm serious."

"I know, KC. You're always serious. If it

weren't for Faith and me, you never would have learned to smile."

KC threw her wadded-up napkin at Winnie, who batted it around, trying to get KC to join her in a game of napkin volleyball. But after a single volley, KC let the napkin land in the ashtray.

KC looked serious. "What I'm saying, Winnie, is that going to Europe is a little more ambitious than just being a counselor at drama camp, like Faith was. Or working in your parents' restaurant, like I did."

"You think so?" Winnie tipped her cup so that a milk mustache decorated her upper lip. She made a face, pushing her nose to one side and sticking out her tongue. "See, KC? In spite of all that culture, I'm still me. Old, demented me."

Finally KC laughed, a goofy, high-pitched giggle. "I missed old, demented you."

"Of course you did. But I'm sure it wasn't so bad to be home all summer. Besides, culture—with a capital C—can be overrated."

"Really?"

"I don't know. Maybe it is, maybe it isn't." Winnie sighed, then pumped herself up again. "Anyway, you made money. And you wanted to make money, right?"

"Everyone wants to make money," KC reflected, "except my parents. They want to live on good vibes." She didn't add that she also *needed* to make money because her parents couldn't afford both her tuition and her dorm. She'd worked all summer at her parents' health food restaurant, plus she'd been a part-time sales clerk, an occasional baby sitter, and (for a few days) a model for a small department store.

"Hey, how was it?" Winnie wanted to know. "Working for your folks, I mean."

"I survived." KC opened her eyes wide and put on a spacey smile. She spoke in a breathy, mocking voice, "Hi, my name is Kahia Cayanne–a name I don't admit to very often. I am your groovy waitperson for the evening. Peace. Love. And enjoy your curried soybean salad."

Winnie howled and stamped her duck shoes. "I love your parents!"

"Of course you do," KC came back. "Now your mom. Your mom is great."

Winnie shrugged, and KC thought back to when she and her parents had picked up Winnie that morning. Unlike the Angeletti family, who hugged and kissed KC as if they were a litter of spaced-out puppies, Winnie had been sitting alone in front of her mom's ultra-modern house, surrounded only by her collection of carpetbags, a pair of roller skates, and an electric wok. KC wished her parents had respected her enough to let her leave for college on her own. Of course, Winnie's divorced mom was a psychologist, so she understood how important things like that were.

"You know how my mom is into giving me so much independence, so I can make my own decisions and my own mistakes." Winnie played with one of her earrings. "I guess that's good, but I still wouldn't mind her calling me Winnie the Pooh every once in while and making me totally embarrassed."

"You always did like to make a public spectacle of yourself," KC teased.

Winnie ran her hands through her short, short hair, and then waved them in the air. "*C'est moi.* That's French for 'If I drink any more coffee I'll start bouncing off the walls.' "

"Winnie, I'd be worried about you if you *weren't* bouncing off the walls." KC checked her freshman orientation brochure and glanced back at Winnie. Their whole first week at U of S would consist of orientation. Not a single class started until the following Monday. "There sure are a lot of orientation activities this week. First I think we need to check in with the housing office and make sure that everything is okay with our rooms. And we should pick up our dorm keys."

"Yes, sir." Winnie saluted. "Shouldn't we go find Faith first? We said we would."

KC put her orientation brochure in her briefcase. "Brooks is helping her move in, so forget about seeing her until she unglues herself from Mr. Wonderful."

"Maybe they'll get unglued permanently," Winnie mused.

"Winnie! How can you say that? Brooks is great."

"Okay, okay." Winnie scooped up a carpetbag containing horror novels, incense, a Walkman, and her roller skates. "But don't you wonder what it would be like to go to college with the boyfriend you've had since ninth grade? I thought college was the time for adventure and all that."

"You'll have enough adventures for all three of us, Win."

Winnie grinned. "I'm sure going to try."

"Come on."

"All right. We'll find Faith later." Winnie slung her carpetbag over her shoulder. She grabbed the last bit of cookie. "Hey, maybe they'll make a mistake and put us in a three-person room after all. Wouldn't that be a terrific surprise?"

"Winnie . . ." KC looked away.

"Okay, I'm coming."

Winnie followed KC past the folk singer and the espresso machine and out into the blinding mountain sunlight. She was always amazed at how together KC could be. Even on the eve of a whole new life, after a whole summer apart, KC was calm and collected. Winnie, on the other hand, was so hyped, she practically bounced like a pogo stick. They both blinked and stared across the street at the athletic facilities clustered on the north end of campus.

Suddenly Winnie stopped. She had missed KC and Faith so badly that summer, it had been like having two empty wells inside her. With Faith it was easy to pick up their friendship exactly where they'd left off. But not with KC. All day Winnie had been feeling like she had to catch up, to remind KC, *Hey! I'm the one who made you chocolate-chip burritos when you found out you couldn't afford leadership camp. I'm the one who shared hundreds of gym classes with you, scores of mall crawls, and at least a dozen all-night talks.*

Winnie faced KC. "KC, do you remember last year when you and I had that big soccer match against Pine Bluff, and I spaced the game, took the phone off the hook, and tried to drown my sorrows in old *Rocky and Bullwinkle* reruns?"

KC nodded.

Winnie pawed fallen leaves with her boot. "I was so bummed because I'd made such a jerk out of myself over Greg Maharis. When Faith couldn't reach me on the phone, she made you drive over and see if I was okay. You got there just in time so I wouldn't miss the game. And we won the division."

"I know this, Winnie," KC insisted.

"I know you know! But I was thinking about that all summer–how I came so close to messing up, but didn't because of you and Faith."

KC softened. "You didn't mess up."

"I almost did." Winnie stamped her foot and continued. "Anyway, I thought about how we'd always been able to depend on each other in high school. And–well, I guess what I'm trying to say is, I'm just glad that we're all going to be here together."

KC was surprised to feel tears sting the corners of her eyes. She really *had* missed Winnie that summer. She'd missed Winnie's unique smarts, her kookiness, her loyalty and affection.

"Okay, the speech is over," Winnie said, getting embarrassed, too. "Come on. Let's go."

KC stuck her arm through Winnie's. "Winnie," she said, her voice trembling a little, "it was a long summer. I really missed you, too."

Together they walked past Sorority Row and toward the U of S football stadium.

Two

Faith was waiting for her roommate. She had unpacked most of her belongings and was pacing from her door to her window and back again. With each footstep echoing down the hall, her pulse picked up and her mouth went dry.

And there were a lot of footsteps. Voices, too. Faith's dorm, Coleridge Hall, was for students of the creative arts. In every corner there seemed to be someone tap dancing, singing, painting, rehearsing, or wandering the halls chewing the end of a pencil. The first floor of young men and the second floor of young women were all studying dance or music, poetry or sculpture, creative writing or theater arts.

"Faith, just relax," Brooks advised as he sat on one of the beds and watched it dip and sag. "Sure, this dorm is a little weird, but it's what you wanted."

"No, no, I like it." Faith said as she continued to pace.

"Did you see that guy downstairs? The one with the orange hair and the earrings?"

"Believe it or not, he's the RA."

"That's your resident assistant?" Brooks laughed. "Okay. It's your dorm, and you said you liked it."

Faith *did* like her dorm. Murals covered the hallway and lobby walls. Every door had something drawn, tacked, or taped onto it. People had converted closets into practice rooms, and one bathroom had been made into a darkroom. In the basement, a makeshift theater had replaced the more standard pool table and video games.

"I just wish my roommate would get here," Faith said, looking out into the hall again. "And what do you think happened to Winnie and KC?"

"They'll be here soon, I'm sure. You three are never too far apart."

Faith hugged her stomach. "I can't stop thinking about my roommate. She's probably a freaky performance artist from San Francisco."

Brooks leaned back and stretched. He wore a soft rugby shirt and hiking pants that had all kinds of pockets. "Maybe she's a tuba player who smokes a pipe."

"A jazz singer with a pet raccoon."

"A modern artist who eats crackers and sardines."

"Wait a minute." Faith stopped and stared down at him. "What about your roommate? Barney Sharfenburger, intriguing chem major from Mount McGraw. What do you think he'll be like?"

"I'm sure he'll be fine." Brooks smiled. "I know we'll get along."

"You do, don't you?"

"I'm not worried. You know me."

"That's one thing I can say for certain, Brooks. I know you. And I bet I saw Barney before on the green," Faith teased. "Did you notice that guy carrying the cage with the white rat?"

"Yeah, he was talking to it."

"That's Barney," they said at the same time, and laughed.

They sat close, listening to the yells floating up from the Frisbee match on the green.

"Don't you wonder what will happen in this room?" Faith whispered, looking around at the mismatched dressers, the battered desks, and the squeaky beds. Coleridge Hall was neither brand-new nor charmingly old. It was just homey and lived-in, which suited Faith just fine. She rested her head against Brooks's shoulder and sighed. "What will happen to us on this campus over the next year?"

Just as Brooks started to hum the old *Twilight Zone* theme, there was a knock at the open door.

Faith shot up. Her heart was beating loudly inside her chest as she stared at her doorway and watched a lithe black girl, wearing a high-cut leotard, shimmery blue tights and a headband, strike a pose in the entrance. The girl had at least a dozen silver bracelets on one wrist, and her feet were bare.

"Hi!" she said in a friendly voice.

"Hi," Faith peeped hopefully.

"I'm Kimberly Dayton."

"I'm Faith Crowley." Faith stood, breathless, looking around for Kimberly's parents and her suitcases. Brooks stood, too.

"I live next door. I'm a dance major," Kimberly explained.

"Oh. Nice to meet you." Faith took a deep breath. "I was trying to figure out why you weren't wearing shoes. I thought maybe it was a new fashion."

Kimberly laughed. "I was just doing a workout."

Brooks came up to her and shook her hand. "I'm Brooks."

"My boyfriend," Faith heard herself announce, surprised at her slightly possessive tone.

"I didn't think he was your roommate," Kimberly teased. "Although in this dorm, you never know."

Faith blushed.

Kimberly laughed. "Anyway, I'm running down to the Seven-Eleven for my Snickers fix. You want anything?"

"No, thanks."

Kimberly started to leave, then turned back. "Are you living in this dorm, too?" she asked Brooks.

Brooks shook his head. "I'm an architecture major. The most creative thing I do is turn on my car stereo," he joked.

Kimberly looked him up and down. "Figures." She winked at Faith and said over her shoulder, "Why is it the cute ones are always architecture majors or pre-law?" Her chuckle echoed down the hall until the door to the stairwell shut.

For a moment Faith and Brooks looked at each other, not quite sure what to say. Then they both laughed.

"Maybe I should have applied for this dorm after all," Brooks teased.

"Brooks!"

Faith pretended to slug him. Soon they were giggling, with Brooks trying to tickle her and Faith standing on his feet. Then things became less giddy. Brooks held her, and their playfulness turned into a kiss—once, twice . . . on the cheek, then on the mouth. Faith let herself melt into the second kiss, until the lovely warmth blocked out everything else. Faith connected with Brooks's happy brown eyes. He smiled at her, then looked out the window toward his dorm. Rapids Hall was in a new complex of wood-sided buildings that were so neat and sterile they were referred to as "The Motels."

"Brooks," Faith assured him, "go ahead and move into your room. I can handle things from here. I won't shrivel up and disappear without you, you know."

"Oh, yeah?" Brooks came back. Suddenly he scooped her up, lifting her until she was almost across his shoulders. "That's not what I hear."

Faith laughed and kicked, her cowboy boots knocking over a shoebox filled with old photos, their high-school yearbook, and postcards. "Let me go!"

Faith was still yelling, kicking, and laughing when she became aware that the door to her room was still open and someone had come in. She expected to see Kimberly again, but soon realized that two people were standing just inside the doorway. She felt a burst of joy at the thought of seeing Winnie and KC.

But it wasn't Winnie and KC. Instead she saw a middle-aged woman and a chubby girl whose fluffy mouse-colored hair dipped to her shoulders.

"Excuse us," said the older woman.

Faith detached herself from Brooks and scrambled to attention. "Yes?"

"Is this room two-nineteen?"

"Yes."

"Well," the older woman said, with a mere hint of formal politeness. "Well, Lauren, here you are."

Faith took a better look at the girl and felt a tug of concern. Lauren had features that were almost too small for her pale, round face. The only part of her that wasn't bland was her eyes, which were a piercing violet. The color was so intense that Faith assumed she wore colored contact lenses. Lauren clutched her expensive leather bag as if someone were trying to steal it away.

"Hello," Faith managed.

"Hello."

"I told you, Lauren," the mother barked. "I told you you wouldn't be comfortable in this dorm." She marched over to the window and looked out, giving Faith's stuffed bear a funny look and moving it aside. "But if you insist on staying here, take the bed by the window. It'll be quieter. And lighter."

But Faith had already put her things on that bed. Brooks took a step toward Lauren and her mother, as if it were his job to settle any dispute over who got which side of the room. Faith managed to cut him off by introducing herself.

"I'm Faith Crowley," she said. "This is my boyfriend, Brooks Baldwin." She held her breath. "Are you my roommate?"

"I'm Janet Turnbell-Smythe, and this is my daughter, Lauren," the mother answered.

Faith looked at Lauren, who didn't say a word.

Lauren's mother walked right past Faith, almost stepping on her foot, then turned back to her daughter. "Lauren, if you really insist on staying at this godforsaken school, why don't you let your father and me buy you a condo?"

Lauren merely stared at the floor. She seemed content to let her mother do everything for her. Finally she spoke. "Yes, I'm your roommate. Most of my things are out in the hall."

Brooks watched open-mouthed as someone who looked like a chauffeur began delivering piece after piece of matching designer luggage. A computer arrived next, then an expensive compact disk player, and finally a TV and microwave oven.

Faith gawked. Lauren's stuff took up three-quarters of the room. She'd been prepared for a prima donna, a genius type, an eccentric, or a flake. She wouldn't have minded a girl who had as many boyfriends as Winnie, one who practiced trombone all night, or even one who made sculpture in the bathroom. But she hadn't been expecting someone like Lauren.

Faith swallowed hard. She tried to control her voice. "Very nice to meet you."

Lauren barely smiled.

Suddenly a voice rang down the hall, ten times louder than the Frisbee game outside or the panicked thunking of Faith's heart.

"Faaaaith!"

"I'm in here!"

It was Kimberly again, wearing shoes this time. She had a sweatshirt tied around her waist. Lauren's mother frowned as Kimberly poked her head inside the doorway and gestured toward the hall.

"Phone call for you, Faith. On the hall phone."

"For me?"

"Yeah. It's someone named Winnie Gottlieb. She says she's an old friend of yours. And she sounds very, very upset."

* * *

Faith found her way to the housing office in record time. She was out of breath and a little sick to her stomach. She, Winnie and KC were sitting on the steps, talking at the same time.

"Thanks for getting over here so fast," Winnie told Faith between gulps and sniffs.

"What happened?"

"I'm sorry. I'm totally and completely sorry."

"What for?"

"I finally get to college and everything starts out as a mess."

"Winnie!"

Winnie flopped over and hugged her knees. "How was I supposed to know they gave your room to someone else if you didn't send in your deposit by July fifteenth?" she wailed.

Winnie's stuff was strewn around her. Freshmen jogged up and down the steps of the housing office, looking eager and nervous on the way in and happily jangling keys on the way out. So far, no one else looked the way Winnie did—like a wreck.

KC gave Winnie's leg a pat. "Winnie, the deadline was on the application form."

"Why didn't you tell me?" Winnie cried. "I was gone all summer. I had other things to worry about. Now I don't have a roommate. I don't even have a *room*! Oh, Faith, you and I and KC should have lived together. I'll die if I can't figure this out."

"Winnie, don't exaggerate. You won't die," KC corrected. "It'll work out."

"But there's a housing shortage. What am I supposed to do? Live in a box in the student union?"

"Don't think about that now," Faith urged her, patting Winnie's back with the flat of her hand. She hugged her. "We'll figure out how to fix this. We always do."

"There's no point in being so emotional about this," KC argued as she flipped through her student handbook. "What we have to do is find you another place to live."

Winnie buried her face in her hands and started crying again. "How are we going to do that?"

"If you'd calm down, we could figure it out."

Winnie knew that KC was trying to be helpful, but she was driving Winnie crazy. Sometimes KC reminded Winnie of her mother. *What are you avoiding this time?* her mother would ask, as she always did when Winnie got into a mess. It didn't matter that Winnie was the world's biggest extrovert; her mother always said she avoided things.

"Whatever you do," Winnie pleaded, "don't call my mom."

"Don't worry," Faith soothed. "We won't."

"I feel so dumb."

"You're *not* dumb."

Winnie took a deep breath and tried to calm herself. Her school guidance counselors always told her how smart she was, and kept asking when she was going to fulfill her potential. If she was so smart, why did she mess things up as badly as this?

"Can you calm down long enough to listen to me?" KC asked.

Winnie shook out her hands and nodded. Meanwhile, Faith handed her a fresh tissue and a stick of peppermint gum.

"Listen," KC advised in her all-business voice, "it says here you can buy someone else's dorm contract."

"What?" Winnie asked.

"What's that, KC?" Faith echoed.

"You wouldn't be able to live with your original roommate. But you would have a dorm room, with some other roommate. KC folded back the page in the handbook and showed it to Winnie. "Some freshmen get here and change their minds about living in the dorm, so they can sell their dorm rental contracts on their own."

Faith lunged across Winnie to look at the handbook. "Really?"

KC gestured back toward the housing office. "We just have to go back into the office and check the bulletin board. I'm sure there will be some cards posted by people who want to get out of their contracts."

"Do you really think so?" Winnie bounded to her feet.

Faith helped Winnie gather her things. They walked back into the housing office, KC leading the way through a mass of freshmen milling around checking handbooks and maps.

Faith hugged Winnie and assured her, "It'll be okay, Win. We'll figure this out. Whatever we have to do, we won't desert you until it's all settled."

"You're such a good friend." Winnie lowered her head onto Faith's shoulder. "Thanks. Oh," she remembered suddenly, "I never even asked you about your roommate. What's she like?"

Faith cringed. "She's . . . okay."

Winnie clutched Faith's arm. "Translated out of Faithspeak, that means she's horrible."

They caught up to KC, who had forged ahead and was studying one of the six on-campus housing bulletin boards. Other students were crowded around, but Winnie saw with relief that there were four cards advertising dorm contracts for sale. She bobbed around the crowd trying to reach the board, but KC plucked off one of the cards and presented it to her.

"Thanks, KC." Winnie grabbed the card,

pressed it to her lips, then let KC lead her and Faith over to the phones.

That night KC thought about what had happened.

It was after she had moved into her single room, neatly made her bed, and organized her desk. She had carefully hung up the new clothes she'd worked all summer to buy. The rest of her room she'd left exactly as she'd found it—nothing taped to the floral wallpaper, no photos from high school or mementos from home.

Lying back on her squeaky single bed, KC considered her old friends. Faith could never understand not needing to decorate your room with things that were old. Just like Winnie couldn't understand not wanting a roommate, or living in a study dorm with a twenty-four-hour quiet rule—especially one that allowed only girls. Faith and Winnie had both admitted that the old dorms were charming, with their big oak staircases and glassed-in porches, but they also agreed that Langston House was not their idea of a homey or fun place to live. That was the problem. They both wanted to make college an extension of high school, with Faith wanting them all to be happy and safe, and Winnie screwing up and looking for fun.

KC knew she wanted something different.

To get along in the world, you had to use your smarts, not your emotions. If it had been up to Winnie and Faith that afternoon, the three of them would have sat on the steps for hours, weeping and consoling each other, until night had fallen and Winnie was out on the street. KC had figured out how to fix the problem, instead of wasting time giving out tissues and patting Winnie's back.

KC still had doubts about attending college with her old friends. Originally she hadn't wanted to. She'd applied to Barton University, a top-notch private school out of state, and the interview was all set. But at the last minute Winnie completely flipped. She had been madly in love with Jeff Talismon, whose family had just decided to move to Texas. When she heard the news, Winnie couldn't eat or sleep or even leave her house. KC couldn't desert Winnie in a state like that, so she postponed her interview. Considering that she needed a scholarship as well, that was a risk she should never have taken. Sure enough, Barton had rejected her, probably because postponing her interview made her look like a flake. And also sure enough, by the following Monday Winnie had recovered and was in love with someone else. Because of her loyalty, KC had blown something vitally important to her future.

She couldn't afford to do that again.

KC had to let Winnie know that things weren't going to be the same as they had been in high school. That night was a good example. The plan was to meet Faith, Brooks, and Winnie and grab pizzas at Luigi's off campus, since they'd missed the dining hall dinner taking care of the contract for Winnie's new room. But KC had decided she didn't want to spend her evening pigging out on pizza, consoling Faith and Winnie, and reminiscing about high school. Not that she didn't still love her old friends, but she wanted to look over her college catalog, figure out which campus organizations would be good to join, and select the most important events to attend during orientation week.

As KC was setting out her date book and orientation brochure, she heard loud footsteps coming down the hallway. Winnie's excited voice mixed with Faith's tired chuckle and the energetic *clop clop* of Brooks's hiking boots. KC considered sticking out her head to remind her friends of Langston's quiet rule, but she didn't. She did nothing. For once, she decided to lay low.

Winnie was laughing as she knocked on KC's door. Ever since she'd found her new dorm room, she had been giddy with relief.

"KC!" she called out. "KC, you've saved me

again. My new room is great. I'm in the wildest dorm on campus. KC, come out and play."

"It's us, KC," called Faith.

KC had a strong impulse to call back, but she held her breath. As Winnie continued to knock, KC stayed put, her heart beating faster as she listened to the conversation on the other side of her door.

"Maybe she went ahead without us," Brooks said.

"Maybe she went to sleep," suggested Faith in a disappointed tone.

Winnie wasn't giving up. "Hey, KC!" She knocked again. "Let's go celebrate solving my first major college trauma. As usual, I couldn't have done it without you! I told you we'd need each other when we got here."

Quiet followed. KC hugged her knees.

"I guess we should go, Winnie. I don't think she's here."

"But I have the feeling she's in there," Winnie insisted.

When KC heard their voices again, they sounded farther down the hall.

"Let's go," Faith said.

"She's probably already over at Luigi's," Brooks added.

Two sets of feet tapped down the stairs.

"KC?" Winnie called one last time.

KC didn't budge. Finally she heard Winnie's rubber duck boots thud and fade away.

KC leaned back against her blank wall and peered out at the dark, deep sky. From her little window she could see her friends traipse out the Langston House front door and head away from the old dorms. Part of her wanted to fly out that window and join them. But another part of her wanted to stay put. If she was going to make something of herself at college, she would have to be tough-minded. She would have to work hard, endure sacrifice, be strong.

She might even have to separate from her old inseparable friends.

Three

"How about that table over there?" she asked Faith. Lauren was trying to smile amid the clanging of silverware and the clunking of coffee cups in the dining commons.

"This table's okay with me if it's okay with you." Faith seemed awkward and unsure as they made their way across the dining hall through a maze of sleepy students.

"The table's perfect," Lauren said too enthusiastically. Faith gave her a funny look, and Lauren felt like an idiot. After all, what could be perfect about a Formica table? "I mean, it's fine. Thank you."

"For what?"

"Excuse me?"

"You said thank you."

"I did? It's nothing. Never mind."

They sat, spread their napkins, and played with their food, while the dining room chatter softened, swelled, and softened again.

"I forgot to get those little things of jam." Faith popped back up, as if she were nervous, too, or couldn't stand sitting with Lauren and wanted to move away. "Want some?"

"Yes, please."

Whipping off her sweater, Faith revealed a T-shirt that said Western High School Drama Festival. "Um, what flavor?"

"Anything is fine."

"I think they only have strawberry and grape," Faith said. "I'll bring both."

"Thank you."

Faith's braid swung as she walked over to the condiment counter. As she watched, Lauren ate too fast and worried about what kind of impression she was making.

Lauren felt as if she were drowning under the foreignness of this huge university. For once in her life, she'd rebelled against her parents by insisting on a large state school in the wild and rugged West. She'd stood up to her mother and her State-Department father and come to a place where she could start fresh, where no one had any preconceptions about Lauren's family or her wealth. But instead of feeling free and joyful, it was as if she'd landed on another planet, one with an atmosphere that made it difficult to breathe.

Faith returned, tossing plastic containers of jam on the table with a loose-limbed ease that Lauren found charming, yet completely unfamiliar. Everything about Faith was so casual, from her lanky frame to her loose golden braid, her soft jeans, and well-worn cowboy boots.

"I brought some honey, too."

"Yes, I see. Thank you."

Lauren sat up very straight and tried to think of something else to say. She'd hoped that Faith might turn out to be someone important. A friend. But after the way they'd met in the room the day before, Lauren feared that it would be a repeat of every other roommate she'd been paired with at a half-dozen different boarding schools: Distant toleration. Politeness. No real closeness or trust.

"Breakfast is pretty good," Faith said, thirstily downing a glass of milk.

Lauren was eating so nervously and tasting so little that she actually had no idea if the food was good or not. She hadn't been prepared for this dining commons experience. She was used to sitting with her hands folded while waiters delivered platters. But U of S dorm residents built pyramids out of English muffins and breakfasted in their bathrobes. By comparison, Lauren was wearing a jacket, matching skirt, and heels. As hard as she was trying to buck her upbringing, she'd spent a half-hour putting on makeup and fixing her hair.

"What are you majoring in?" Faith asked a few minutes later, as if she were making another attempt to start a half-hearted conversation.

"Creative writing." Lauren didn't add, *I love reading and writing because I can sit at my desk alone, instead of painfully trying to start conversations like this one*. She looked out the window at the distant mountains. "The mountains in most of the places I've lived are like little rolling hills compared to the ones here."

"Really?" Faith scrambled up and then sat down again, her legs folded beneath her. "Where did you grow up?"

Lauren cleared her throat. "No one place, really. I've lived all over the world. The place I lived the longest was New York City."

Faith put down her toast. "Seriously?"

Lauren nodded, not sure what she had said to inspire such interest. To her, travel wasn't glamorous. It meant never being around long enough to relax and fit in, never making real friendships because she was always preparing to leave.

Faith blurted. "Even Winnie, my friend who went to Europe, has never been to New York. Have you seen plays on Broadway?"

"Yes."

"Will you tell me about them sometime?"

"Sure. If you want."

Faith brightened and seemed to relax. "Can I ask you one thing?"

"Of course."

"Do people there get mugged all the time?"

"Where?"

"In New York City."

Lauren couldn't help a tiny smile. "Once in a while. But not all the time."

Faith looked down at her tray. When she raised her face again she looked embarrassed. "Was that a dumb, hick question? About getting mugged?"

A drop of reassurance trickled through Lauren. She was the one who felt like a hick. "No. My mother thinks people out here still wear six-shooters and eat bear grease. I guess it's easy to assume things about people you don't know."

They smiled at each other—their first genuine, tentative, it's-okay-I'm-as-nervous-as-you-are smile.

"I know my mother was kind of weird when I moved in," Lauren finally admitted. "I'm sorry."

"It's not your fault."

"She's staying at a hotel in town all through orientation week. I can't wait until she leaves."

"Don't worry about it."

"Thanks." Lauren was starting to feel a hint of hope when Faith looked up, then began grinning and waving her napkin.

"Here come my two best friends from high school. The tall one is KC. The one in the boxer shorts is Winnie."

KC cut through the crowd, striding with purpose and forward drive. She was beautiful, and dressed conservatively in a sweater and pleated skirt. At least half a dozen guys dropped their forks to stare at her as she walked by.

Winnie wore a hooded sweatshirt, boys' boxer shorts, high-tops, and floppy socks. Although she was small, she had a terrific figure. When they reached Faith's table, the Walkman draped around Winnie's neck gave off a distant, tinny ping of rap music.

Winnie and KC stood for a moment, gawking at Lauren. Faith quickly made introductions.

"Good morning, Lauren. Nice to meet you," KC said.

Something about KC's elegant crispness reminded Lauren of saleswomen in expensive stores. "Nice to meet you, too," she whispered.

KC sat down and emptied her tray, which held

more orientation flyers than food. Her breakfast consisted of coffee, sausages, and a frosted chocolate doughnut. Meanwhile, Winnie, who had no tray, stayed standing behind Faith and rested her chin on the top of Faith's head.

"Hi, crazy person," said Faith, trying to look up.

"Where's our Mr. Brooks?" asked Winnie.

"He took the early library tour."

"Without you? I hope this isn't the start of a new trend. I had to surprise KC and practically drag her to breakfast with me. She still won't admit who she was sneaking around with last night."

"Winnie, I told you. I went to sleep early," KC said.

"Yeah, yeah," Winnie teased. "I guess it's possible in that morgue you live in. Well, guess what—I found out more about my new abode, Forest Hall. It's the jock party house." She tugged Faith's braid. "I think I'll mess up more often."

"Sure, Winnie." Faith laughed.

"Of course most of the residents haven't moved in yet. But I can tell from the shocking and disgusting things scribbled in the stairwells that it's my kind of place."

"What about your roommate?" Faith asked.

"I haven't met her yet. Her name's Melissa."

Winnie's earrings swung as she looked at the other three. "I found out she's from Springfield."

KC looked surprised. "Really? A townie?"

"I guess." Winnie snatched one of the orientation brochures off KC's tray. "Study workshop? Whoa! KC, are you going to that?"

"I am."

"Forget the study workshop. The toga party sounds much more my speed."

KC looked at Lauren. "Winnie's so smart, she doesn't need to study."

Lauren didn't know how to reply. She felt like a stranger at a close family reunion.

Winnie filled in the pause. "I've just perfected the art of the last-minute cram. Maybe I should give an orientation workshop on that. Winnie Gottlieb's art of procrastination."

KC laughed.

"Well, I want to go to the ice cream social tonight," Faith commented. "And canoeing on Mill Pond. I think that's on Friday."

"Well, right now I'm going for a jog." Winnie began to stretch.

"Are you running alone?" Faith asked. "Be careful."

"Yes, Mother Faith."

Lauren forced herself to sit forward and contribute something. "You shouldn't jog through that pioneer graveyard,'' she cautioned, but as soon as she said it, she felt stupid. There was an old pioneer cemetery in the middle of the campus, and her mother acted as if it were full of outlaws waiting for someone to ambush.

''Ooooo, ooooo, scary!'' Winnie exclaimed.

Lauren felt a warm blush spread across her cheeks. For an awful moment she could feel all three girls staring at her. But then Winnie reached out and touched her shoulder.

''I'm teasing! Thanks for telling me. Actually, I'm the kind of person who needs warnings like that.'' Winnie propped her foot up on a chair and retied her sneaker. ''It's really nice to meet you. And since you're rooming with Faith, you'll have to put up with motor-mouth me, too. I hope that's okay.''

''Of course. Thanks.''

As soon as Winnie left, there was an awkward silence again.

As if she had read Lauren's thoughts, Faith leaned closer. ''Listen, Brooks is in the Honors College, and they have a special orientation meeting this morning. I'm going with him. Do you want to come?''

''I'm supposed to go over to Sorority Row this morning and meet my mother,'' Lauren explained.

"She wants to introduce me to someone at the Tri Beta house. Rush is this week."

KC lifted her face. One dark curl hung down over her forehead and there was a speck of chocolate frosting on her chin, but other than that, she looked perfect. "You're going to rush a sorority?"

Lauren nodded.

"Tri Beta?"

"Yes."

"I read about it in one of our orientation brochures. It sounds like the best sorority on campus."

"It could be."

KC was staring, as fascinated by Lauren's talk about the sorority as Faith had been earlier about New York City. But KC's dark eyes had none of the unguarded sweetness that Faith's had. They were focused with ambition and purpose.

Then Faith noticed Brooks on the other side of the big picture window, holding a bag from the university bookstore and rapping on the glass. Faith signaled to him and started stacking her dishes, as did KC. Lauren watched them and did the same.

As they were making their way out, with a pause to bus their trays, KC crossed in front of Lauren and looked at her with a piercing, inquisitive look. "Lauren, would you mind if we walked across campus together? I have to go past Sorority Row to get to my waitressing job."

"That's a great idea," Faith said. "You two can get to know each other! Lauren, tell KC about New York City."

"I don't mind walking by myself," Lauren assured KC.

"Of course, Lauren. I'd love to hear all about New York," KC said as they strolled out into the crisp mountain morning. She waved goodbye to Faith and Brooks. "I'd like to talk to you about a lot of things."

"Oh," Lauren breathed, uplifted and surprised. "Yes. I'd like that, too."

"The key word in Honors College is dedication."

Brooks kept a protective arm around Faith as he listened to Dr. DeBrod, dean of the U of S Honors College, give his orientation speech. They were in Hendricks Hall, an auditorium with the standard state and national flags, plus a large oil painting of Yellowstone Park. What weren't standard were the four hundred freshmen who filled the seats. They were supposedly among the brightest, the most promising, and the most intellectually curious in their class.

"As you all know," Dr. DeBrod lectured,

"Honors College is a liberal arts school within the university where we bring motivated students together with our most exceptional faculty. Classes are small, and study is in depth. It's a challenge, but you can expect great returns."

"Brooks," Faith whispered, "this sounds great."

Brooks nodded. "I know."

Dr. DeBrod waited out a ring of microphone feedback, then went on with his talk. "Many of our Honors graduates are now prominent film directors, art historians, and scientists. You can all contribute to your area of interest if you are committed to excellence. And we're here to help you do just that, by stimulating you and making you strive even harder."

Brooks shifted in his seat and his mind drifted off. When he'd applied to Honors College the past January, he hadn't given his commitment to excellence much thought. He hadn't given this whole idea much thought. His father had suggested it and Brooks's grades were good enough, so the application went in. A lot of things in Brooks's life had started out as easily as that. Student government, mountain climbing, Eagle Scouts. Even his relationship with Faith had started without effort and progressed with ease.

Dr. DeBrod was smiling. "Let me finish by saying that college is a unique and exciting time. I encourage you to explore new things, to get involved in clubs and organizations. And please remember that while orientation week is a carefree time for you to get acquainted with the university, next week is the beginning of your studies. I wish all of you the best, and I hope to meet many of you individually. Now let me introduce Professor Harrington, one of our distinguished faculty members. He'll speak to you about the film studies program he started last year."

When Dr. DeBrod stepped down, Faith leaned toward Brooks and whispered, "Now I know why you applied for this." She sighed. "Maybe I should try to get into Honors College sophomore year."

"Definitely," Brooks agreed. "It does sound great, doesn't it."

Faith nodded and rested her head on his shoulder.

Brooks put his arm around her while a stark, almost scary realization washed over him.

This wasn't high school anymore.

KC guided Lauren to one side of a narrow bike path, allowing cyclists in helmets and sleek racing outfits to speed by. They were approaching Morton Library, passing the huge radar dish that transmitted KRUS, the college radio station.

"So even if someone got accepted to a sorority this year . . ." KC prompted.

"Were offered a bid," Lauren clarified in a soft, breathy voice. "That's what they call it, when they invite you to join."

"Offered a bid."

"Right. My mother's been telling me about this since I was twelve. The Greek system–the sororities and fraternities–is nationwide. They do community service, but sororities and fraternities are mainly social organizations. My mom says a sorority is a sisterhood, and that the other sorority girls will be your friends for your entire life. But you have to be invited in. That's what rush and pledging are all about. It's the time to select new members." They passed the library windows and saw rows of computer terminals inside.

KC backtracked. "So even if you were invited to join–given a bid–you still wouldn't live in the sorority house until next year?"

Lauren nodded. "You would still be a member during freshman year, though, and you'd participate in sorority functions. You just wouldn't be allowed to move out of the dorms until you were a sophomore."

KC couldn't get enough information out of Lauren. She'd realized that although Lauren had seemed quiet, if she was prodded a little she could be almost as good a talker as Winnie. But where Winnie babbled nonsense and jokes, Lauren was a gold mine of important information. She'd told KC about her summers spent on exclusive East Coast islands and her vacations in London and Japan. KC would have given anything for experiences like those.

KC and Lauren sped up, heading around the information booth and passing the sculpture garden and the Women's Center.

"Do you think Tri Beta is the best house to pledge?" KC asked.

"That's what my mother thinks." Lauren was slightly out of breath. Her milky, soft skin was pinking up over her neck and her round cheeks. "My mother's active in the Tri Beta Alumni. She assumes that's where I'll end up."

"Do you think you'll like it?"

Lauren was silent for a moment. "My mom says being in a sorority is a good way to meet people."

"So a sorority is sort of like a club."

"Actually," Lauren admitted, "my mom's expression was 'social contacts.' Sorority sisters make good social contacts."

"Contacts?"

"Contacts for careers, for the future." Lauren shrugged. They were approaching the athletic facilities at the north end of campus.

KC nodded.

"My mom was a Tri Beta back east," Lauren explained. "She's connected to people out here because of the house. This morning she had breakfast with a Tri Beta woman who runs a bank here. I don't agree with my mother about very much, but the idea of a club, a bunch of friends—sisters—is appealing. Like you and Winnie and Faith."

KC doubted that any sorority had members as different as she, Winnie, and Faith were. Especially a house like Tri Beta. She knew that Lauren was being modest in not mentioning that Tri Beta was *the* sorority on campus. KC had heard that Tri Beta housed the richest and best-connected girls. And connections were important: KC knew that if she'd had a father or an aunt who'd given money to the Barton alumni fund, Barton would have accepted her even without an interview.

Leaving the football stadium behind them, KC and Lauren took a footpath that passed the tennis courts and finally left the campus. It was another two blocks before downtown, where The Beanery sat between Magpie Records and Zappy's Xerox Center. Two blocks of stately houses that made up Sorority and Fraternity Row.

KC stopped in front of the first house and stared. Three stories of elegant white wood loomed over her. There was a sun porch and a little balcony.

Two girls in skirts and sweaters were tacking up paper fish kites around the entrance. Rock music blasted from the first floor.

Her heart beat faster. "So, rush is this week, during orientation?" KC hinted, before she and Lauren had to go their separate ways.

Lauren looked a little lost. She turned her face away from the sorority girls. "It starts tomorrow night."

KC checked her watch. She couldn't dawdle, not if she wanted to make it to work on time. Nonetheless, she had to make a decision. She'd missed out on Barton, but maybe this was another chance to get where she wanted to go. "What if I rushed, too? Would you want to do it together?"

A glow spread over Lauren's chubby face. "You'd really want to go through rush with me?"

"Of course I would," KC decided. "I don't know anything about sororities. You'd be helping me no end."

"Really?" Lauren beamed, looking shyly at KC, then back toward the sorority girls. "All right. I mean, yes. Oh, yes! Thank you. That would be wonderful!"

"Thank *you*," KC said.

She touched Lauren's arm, then ran all the way to her waitressing job.

Four

The Welcome Freshmen ice cream social was held in Swedenborg House, the oldest structure on campus. The shingles of the house had recently been painted white, and the inside was lit with chandeliers.

Faith, Winnie, Brooks, and Brooks's roommate, Barney Sharfenburger, had walked by it several times that day. It was their second full day on campus and the four of them had traipsed over to the campus police station, where they'd registered Faith's and Brooks's bikes, and then had gone downtown to locate the movie theaters and the outdoor-equipment stores. Finally they'd gone with Winnie to the registrar's office, since she had missed preregistration and had to get a special sign-up time to register for her classes. During all that walking, however, KC had been strangely absent.

"Look at that," Winnie couldn't help mentioning to Faith as they sat finishing their ice cream. They were squeezed together at a table between the crowded ice cream counter and a circle of arty types from Faith's dorm.

"What, Win?"

"KC just glommed onto Lauren. Again."

Winnie gestured toward KC, who was off near the punch bowl, intently quizzing Lauren. Faith knew what Winnie meant. All day KC and Lauren had been hanging out together, shopping on The Strand, the fanciest area in Springfield.

"That was some dress KC bought with Lauren today," Faith marveled. "I guess she's supposed to get dressed up for the first night of rush tomorrow."

"What's the big deal about a boring black dress?" Winnie rolled her eyes. "You'd think for a hundred and sixty bucks you could at least get solid gold spangles."

"Come on." Faith elbowed her. "It was really nice of Lauren to let KC use her credit card."

"I guess. I mean, it's none of my business." Winnie stared at the other freshmen. "I don't care what kind of wardrobe KC has."

"You know, I like Lauren," Faith decided. "I think it's good to get to know people who are new and different."

"Yeah, yeah." Suddenly Winnie threw off her gloom and grinned. "Speaking of new, I think I'll see if I can strike up at least one thrilling conversation. I hate getting dressed up for nothing." Winnie bolstered herself for another moment and pinched her cheeks. "You okay on your own?"

"Of course," Faith said.

Winnie patted her. "Well, I'm sure I'm about to have the time of my life. But if I don't, I think I'll go back to my dorm early." She took a deep breath and disappeared into the crowd.

Faith stood alone for a while, listening to the muffled music. She wasn't sure why she had bothered to dress up for the ice cream social, either. She was wearing Brooks's favorite outfit: an embroidered blouse he'd given her on her last birthday and her best Levi's. But Brooks had gone off to get some more ice cream and seemed to have gotten lost in the crowd. Winnie could no longer be seen. KC and Lauren were deep in what looked like a private conversation.

Faith decided to make a move on her own. She shuffled closer to the arty Coleridge group, and for a while stood awkwardly outside their lively circle.

Kimberly finally noticed her and stepped aside to include Faith in the conversation.

"This is my next-door neighbor, Faith," Kimberly announced to the others.

"Hi, everyone," Faith said, smiling. Besides Kimberly, there were Kimberly's roommate, Freya, an exchange student from Germany who was an opera major; Beth, an art major who wore white lipstick, handmade sandals and a man's suit jacket; and Dante, who had a precise, theatrical voice and wore suspenders and an antique tie.

"Kimberly told me you're studying drama. Dante's a theater arts major, too," Freya said.

"Great." Faith smiled at Dante.

Dante posed like a mime leaning on an invisible lamp post. "It's true. I'm a drama freak."

Kimberly patted him. "Dante was just telling us about the plays he did his last year in high school. One was a Beckett play, where he had to be in a trash can for the whole performance."

"A trash can?" Faith repeated.

Dante nodded. "For the whole play. A lot of people didn't get it. But it was a great experience."

"I guess."

Kimberly went on. "And the other was a Sam Shepard play."

"What!" Faith heard herself gasp. Even she knew that Shepard's plays were avant-garde and very intense. In some there were scenes with dead animals, or people walking around naked, shouting obscenities.

"It was no big deal," Dante said.

Faith couldn't stop herself from gaping.

Dante held up his hands. "We didn't do it for the whole school. It was a special workshop production. We all stayed up until midnight for two weeks rehearsing it."

Faith was impressed. At Lewis and Clark they didn't go much further than *The Sound of Music* and *The Mousetrap*. She'd thought it adventurous to stage a fistfight between Kate and Petruchio in her *Taming of the Shrew* scene. Still, she'd never taken the kind of daring step that Dante was talking about.

"I'd like to hear more about your productions," Faith told Dante. "I'd love to borrow some scripts to read sometime."

"Sure. Hey, Faith," Dante added in his low, self-conscious voice, "there's a production getting started here this week. They're holding auditions and interviews tomorrow in the University Theater."

"Really?"

Dante nodded. "Yeah. Well, it's nothing like what I did in high school, just this corny little musical with a student director. They're doing *Stop the*

World, I Want to Get Off. And from what I've heard, the fact that it's not a major production means that freshmen might actually get a chance to be in it. You have to get there before ten-thirty in the morning to sign up."

"They need dancers, so I'm auditioning, too," Kimberly volunteered. "Faith, you're interested in backstage work, not performing, right?"

Faith nodded. "Directing, too, I guess. I want to do a little of everything."

"Hey, that's great. Good for you," Beth suddenly interrupted. "I was afraid all the other women in our dorm wanted to be starlets or belly dancers." Beth put her hands on her lapels. "No offense, Kimberly."

Kimberly laughed.

Faith turned her attention to Beth. "So you're an art major?"

"Well," Beth said, "actually I'm more interested in women's politics, but I'm good at art and I thought it might be a powerful way to get my ideas across. See, a long time ago I went to see an exhibit that was a series of table settings created by women artists. No one used to think women's crafts were anything special. Of course, it took a woman to think of putting the exhibition together. You know what I mean?"

Faith was about to tell Beth that she did know

what she meant, when suddenly she spotted Brooks. He was standing at the corner of the ice cream counter, talking and laughing with a group of people dressed in hiking boots and climbing shorts. They were from his dorm and appeared to share Brooks's passion for outdoor pursuits. A girl was offering Brooks a taste of her ice cream.

"Oh, excuse me," Faith apologized to Beth. "I'd love to talk to you again. But I have to go." She gestured to Brooks. "That's my boyfriend. It's really nice to meet you. I'll see you around the dorm, I'm sure."

As she threaded her way through the crowd Faith kept her eyes on Brooks, who had just seen her and was waving her over. She joined the group and slipped her arm around Brooks's waist.

Winnie left the ice cream social early. She ran back to her dorm, racing faster and faster until her sides hurt, her legs ached, her heart worked doubletime and her lungs begged for air.

Her mother always said she exercised too much. She told Winnie that it was an addiction, that Winnie did it so she wouldn't have to think. Well, right then Winnie didn't want to think—about the summer that had just ended, about KC, about her classes, or about her invisible roommate, the mysterious Melissa McDormand, who had spelled out *hello* in jelly beans on Winnie's bed but who hadn't been seen since. As far as Winnie was concerned, too many people had deserted her.

As Forest Hall came into view, Winnie decided she didn't even want to think about her new dorm. The sterile, motel unfriendliness of it. Every floor, every stairwell, every room was so exactly the same that Winnie could picture herself getting lost and ending up in the wrong room.

But she had to think about her dorm, because soon she was in front of it, where a noisy free-for-all was going on. Rock music blasted as guys played keepaway with a Frisbee. Their leaps and grabs and staggers and falls were silly and daring at the same time.

Winnie stopped. She wanted to join them, to be really carefree and uninhibited, to have the fun she pretended to want so badly. But instead she put her fists in her pockets and bent her head down, as if she were deep in contemplation.

Midway across the front lawn of the dorm, Winnie heard a shout.

"Look out!"

Winnie looked up. A Frisbee floated at eye level, hovering like a blue flying saucer.

Instinctively, she reached out. The spiraling disk floated down over her ringed index finger and settled like a bird.

Then the night exploded.

"Hey, she's got it. Grab her!"

Strong arms gripped her around her waist and swung her off her feet, like she was a beach ball about to be catapulted into the next county. The Frisbee was knocked from her hand and went rolling. Winnie felt herself being passed from one pair of arms to another. She thought that she was going to end up on the cold, dewy grass, but then, surprisingly, the last pair of arms locked around her waist and gently steadied her so that she wouldn't fall.

"You okay?" asked a voice that apparently went along with the arms.

Winnie gasped for air. "I think so."

He laughed, and Winnie felt composed enough to turn her face up and look. When she did her legs went wobbly. The boy who was holding her had large, deep-set eyes and thick black hair clipped short on the sides but flopping over his forehead. He was wearing a green T-shirt, well-worn Levi's, and moccasins. Around his wrist was a piece of twine twisted like a bracelet and he wore a single earring, a tiny, barely visible dot of marbley blue in one ear.

"Hi," Winnie managed to say after she realized she had been staring at him for much too long.

"Hello."

The Frisbee game, meanwhile, had bypassed them. The chasing, screaming hordes were running down toward the other end of the lawn.

"That's the risk of walking through the middle of the game," he said. His voice sounded laid-back and full of humor.

"Did I walk through the middle?" Winnie asked. "With Frisbee it's kind of hard to tell."

"It is, isn't it?" He smiled and began to stroll off the grass. He seemed to be heading toward Forest Hall.

Winnie walked with him. "There's no fifty-yard line or home plate or anything, I mean. No basket."

"No net."

"No goal."

"No finish line."

"No water wheel with elves."

"No what?"

Winnie realized she sounded totally nuts. "At the miniature golf course in my home town, on the final hole you have to hit the ball through into a water wheel with three elves."

He laughed. "My name's Josh."

Winnie almost said, *So's mine*. Then some clarity returned. "I'm Winnie."

"Are you a freshman?"

"Yes. Are you?"

"Yup."

They walked over to the dorm patio, where Josh drew up his long legs and sat down. He tossed his hair back and invited Winnie to sit down next to him.

"Do you live in Forest?"

Winnie nodded.

"I hear it's a pretty wild place. Or it will be when everybody moves in."

"What are you going to study?"

Josh picked up a stray bottle cap and tossed it in the air. "Computers."

Winnie knew that a lot of people were interested in computers—KC wanted one, and Lauren had one. Still, she thought Josh looked more like a guy who wrote poetry or played the synthesizer.

"What about you?"

"Huh?"

"You," Josh repeated. "What are you going to study? Do you have a major?"

"A major?"

"Yeah. You know, field of study. Interest. Related to future job."

Winnie liked the teasing tone in his voice. It gave her the courage, for once, to tell the whole truth. "Oh, that. Sure. History, psychology, architecture, anthropology, special education, environmental studies, all of the above, none of the above."

"The old undeclared."

"That's an understatement." Now Winnie was embarrassed, and wished she hadn't admitted she wasn't sure. She felt like she should have said, *Yes, I'm majoring in engineering. I'll get my undergraduate degree and then I'll go for my masters and then I'll get an entry level job with the city of so and so, and move up from there.*

"It's nothing to be ashamed of," Josh said, nudging her with his shoulder.

"I just feel like I should decide."

He turned to face her, looking truly interested. "Why? Why should you decide right now? You're only a freshman."

"I know. I just wish I was overwhelmingly talented at something," she confessed. "I wish that I was a great singer or a brilliant mathematician, or that I could speak Japanese. I wish I had some burning interest—something I had to do or die in the attempt, that kind of thing."

"You'll find it. Isn't that what college is about? I *think* I want to do something with computers, but it wouldn't matter if I didn't. College should be as much about figuring out what you want to do as it is about learning how to do it. Nothing ever turns out the way you think it will, anyway."

"You really think that?"

"Sure. I say, be prepared for whatever you think might happen." He smiled. "And then wait around a while and see."

Winnie wanted to throw her arms around Josh's neck for saying that. Of course, she'd wanted to throw her arms around him since she'd first laid eyes on him.

Josh sighed and leaned back. "I'll tell you, though, as much as I know what I want to study, I would still like to take a year off. Maybe see the whole United States. Ride around on a motorcycle. See all the back roads, and the big cities, too. Get to know different people—that's my idea of a great education."

"It is," Winnie quickly agreed. Unable to stop herself, she added, "I spent this whole summer in France."

"You did? How was it?"

"Incredible! I lived with a family, but I was still almost totally on my own. I did whatever I wanted. I met lots of different people, like you said." She hesitated, then put on a sexy smile. "I had some real adventures."

"The school of real life, huh?"

She bit her lip. "You could say that."

"I bet."

For a moment they stared at each another and

Winnie felt paralyzed. She knew that she was already a little shaky because of all the changes involved in going to college. Falling head over heels after knowing him for five minutes wasn't going to help. If anything, it was a recipe for disaster.

Instead of sweeping her up in his arms, Josh clapped his hands against his thighs and stood up. He tousled the top of Winnie's hair. "I'd really like to talk some more, but I've got to go in," he explained. "Jerry, the RA here, has one of those NEXT computers. He said he'd let me experiment with it if I caught him before eleven."

Winnie hopped up.

Josh stalled for a moment and stood with his hands on his hips. "What room are you in?"

"Uh . . . um . . ." She couldn't remember.

"Well listen." Josh put up his hand in a no-problem gesture. "I'm in one-forty-one. We should eat breakfast together sometime."

Suddenly it dawned on her. For some dumb reason it hadn't really sunk in until just that moment. "You mean you live in Forest, too? You live in *this* dorm?"

"Yeah, in 141. Maybe we'll run into each other at some of this orientation stuff. There's a free movie almost every night at the media center. And isn't there canoeing or something this Friday on Mill Pond?"

"There is?" She tried to figure out whether he was asking her out, or if it was one of those general "see you around" kind of goodbyes.

"Anyway, I'll see you. Are you going to the dorm toga party?" He laughed. "I guess we're supposed to wear togas."

Winnie wasn't going to admit that she wouldn't miss that dance now if her life depended on it.

Josh folded his arms, then nodded. "See you soon."

"Bye."

"It was good to talk to you."

"You, too."

Then Josh was gone. "Oh, God!" Winnie suddenly yelled, clapping her hands over her mouth so that she wouldn't make too much noise.

She ran into the lobby of Forest Hall and down an orange-carpeted hallway, wondering if Josh was a dream. Then Winnie saw something that made her stop in her tracks.

It wasn't much. Just a door. A plain, cream-colored door with a diagonal orange stripe. Nothing to make her want to leap out of her jogging shoes and kiss the sky—except that it was room 141, Josh's room 141. She lived in 152. Josh's room was less than a hundred feet from hers.

Winnie galloped those hundred feet to her

own door. When she'd imagined coed dorms, somehow she never thought they'd be this completely coed! Of course the girls and guys had separate lavatories, but there was no way she wouldn't see Josh again—not when he lived on the same floor.

Winnie slipped her key in the lock and opened her own door. She was in the perfect mood to meet her roommate now: no nerves, no insecurity about KC or about living in a building full of strangers, just high excitement and a clear sense that everything in the world was going to work out.

But as Winnie reached for the light switch, her hand froze in midair. She realized with a sigh that the girl she really wanted to share this discovery with—the other occupant of room 152—was sound asleep. Winnie slipped inside, closing the door behind her, and let her eyes adjust to the dark until she was able to make out the shape of snoozing Melissa just barely outlined by the moonlight.

"Hi, Melissa," Winnie whispered. "Nice to meet you."

Winnie tiptoed to her bed, slithering out of her shoes, running shorts, tights, leotard, and bra. She let each piece of clothing clack or whoof as it hit the floor. She barely thought about Melissa sleeping so peacefully in the other bed. At that moment she wouldn't have cared if her roommate had turned out to be a vampire, a kleptomaniac, or a human-sized slug.

All Winnie could think about was Josh. Josh would soon be in his bed, too. So close—just five doors down the hall.

Five

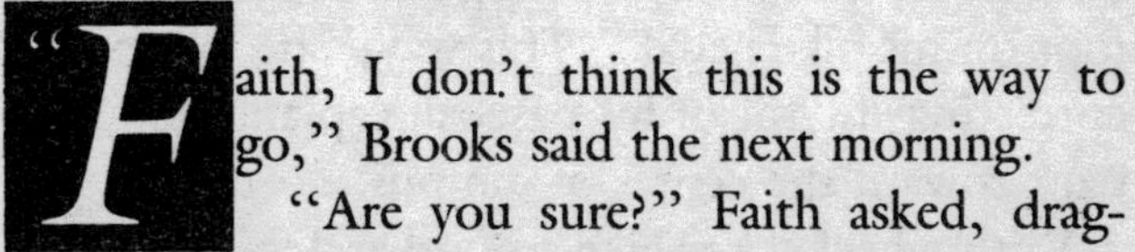

"Faith, I don't think this is the way to go," Brooks said the next morning.

"Are you sure?" Faith asked, dragging her loafer along the ground to slow down her bicycle. She blew on her cold hands, then plucked the campus map from her new book bag, then secured the bag back in the basket of her bike. "I think I'm right," she said.

Brooks, who stood next to her astride his ten-speed, took the map. Over breakfast he had decided to accompany Faith to the auditions at the University Theater. He thought it would be a great opportunity to see more of the campus.

"See, here's Mill Pond, and just in front is the

University Theater," he said, gesturing toward the map.

"Wait," she told him. "Did you see a sign by that last building? Was that Churchill Hall?"

"I don't think so," Brooks insisted.

They stood there, blocking the bike path. Faith still thought she was right. If they just rode straight ahead, then went along the edge of Mill Pond, past the boathouse and the stretch of water where the crew team worked out, they would reach the theater.

Brooks put the map in his pocket and cocked his foot on his bike pedal. "This way," he instructed, correcting the tilt of his baseball cap and gesturing back toward the center of campus.

Faith wheeled her bike around and followed. After all, Brooks was the pathfinder, the one who carried a compass in his pocket.

"How's it going with Lauren?" Brooks asked, changing the subject.

Faith pretended to cut in front of him with her bike, which made him lean back and practically do a spin on one wheel. "I was just thinking about her," she said.

They sped up, coasting down a slope behind the library. Gargoyles were on the top corners of the building. Faith and Brooks both stuck out their tongues at the stone monsters, then rode past. Just ahead was a big, modern building with a box office in front. It had to be the University Theater, Faith thought.

Faith answered as they pedaled. "I like her more and more. She's different from us. And you know what?"

Brooks held his arm out to warn her to slow down. They were nearing the end of the bike path and hopped off to walk their cycles down a dirt trail.

"What?" Brooks asked.

"I like the fact that she's different. It's really great to be meeting all these new people."

Brooks nodded. "I think so, too." Then he frowned and stopped to check their location again. A perplexed look came over his face.

"That's not the University Theater, is it?" Faith cried, checking her watch. "That's the concert hall!"

"You're right." He sighed. "Shoot. I saw that building and I was—"

"I thought you were sure!" Faith exploded. She was surprised by her sudden anger. "Brooks, I have to be there in a few minutes." She took the map from Brooks and checked it to find her destination. The University Theater was behind the concert hall and Mill Pond. But it looked like the bike path led to it in a long, roundabout squiggle.

"Look, I'm sorry," Brooks argued. "You'll make it. Just go ahead on foot." Brooks got off his bike and pointed toward another path that led behind the concert hall and had a No Bikes Allowed sign. "Cut through there. I'll lock the bikes up and find you."

"Okay." She got off her bike. "Thanks."

"Hurry up."

Faith began running, hoping to make up for the lost time and to cool her anger. She wasn't used to blowing up at Brooks, and it left her with an awful, unsettled feeling. She sped up and stopped a man who looked like a professor.

"Is that the theater building?" she prayed.

"Next one," he called out as he hurried on.

Faith turned and saw it. "Thank you."

Faith ran quickly down the path. Soon she was trotting up the stone steps of the University Theater. Sound spewed out the open double doors; inside she could hear a piano tinkling and people clearing their throats, humming, and rehearsing lines. Further inside, someone was calling off names in a strong, authoritative voice.

Taking a deep breath, Faith entered.

The old lobby had thin, worn carpet patterned with big flowers. The room was cluttered with folding chairs. Most of the performers hovered around a small bulletin board. People were pacing and laughing, and some were smoking nervously. Dante, the drama major Faith had met at the ice cream social, was doing a headstand. Another actor held his nose while repeating a tongue twister. Faith saw Kimberly, who was wearing black tights and sweatshirt that said Oregon Modern Dance.

But Faith didn't stop to talk. Instead she cut through the cigarette smoke and made her way over to the bulletin board. There were notices about scholarships and apprenticeships, but no sign-up sheets.

"Oh, no," she gasped out loud. Why had she ever listened to Brooks?

"Is there anyone else who signed up to sing?" yelled the same strong, quick voice that Faith had heard calling out names as she came in.

Faith turned around. The young man in charge was wearing a tweed sport jacket, rumpled cords, a bolo tie in the shape of a musical note, and wire-rimmed glasses.

Faith caught up to him. "Excuse me. Did you take down the sign-up sheet already?"

"We're almost out of time," he told her without sympathy. "Dancers were supposed to show up early." Not waiting for a response, he looked out over the crowd again and projected. "Christopher will have callbacks on Saturday. He'll post the list tomorrow."

"What time?" a girl begged in a panicked voice.

"Whenever Sir Christopher can fit it into his schedule. It'll be posted. Thank you, one and all. Pick up your trash on the way out."

He started to walk away. Faith was so disappointed, she thought she might start to cry. She surprised herself by actually grabbing at his coat sleeve.

"Wait. I was supposed to be here by ten-thirty, and it's ten-twenty-eight. I got lost on the way here. *Please.*"

He stopped at Faith's tug, looked puzzled, then finally checked his watch.

"Right you are," he admitted, then he sighed. "Oh, well, why not? But I can't promise Sir Christopher—he's our student director—and the choreographer will watch more than a few steps. Christopher has another appointment, probably with the Interfraternity Council."

"But I don't want to dance."

"The girls playing the daughters *have* to dance."

Faith hugged her body bag. "I don't want to perform. I can do almost anything backstage. I want to work wherever you need me," she said.

He was already walking away, then made a U-turn without missing a beat. A moment later he was facing Faith again, and his irritated expression had turned to a big smile. "I'm Merideth." He stuck out a hand to shake. "I know it's a weird name. My parents were free thinkers."

"I'm Faith. I know it's a normal name. I guess my parents were normal thinkers."

He smiled. "Okay. 'Can do anything backstage,' " he wrote on his clipboard. "You're a gift from heaven," he said, looking up. "You must be a freshman."

Faith nodded, wondering if that was a problem. "I've had a lot of experience in high school, though," she explained. "Nothing too unusual or experimental, but I work hard. If I've never done it before, I can always learn."

"I like that attitude."

"Thanks."

The nervous auditioners, who had been collecting near the door with their coats on and dance bags in hand, all seemed to turn at the same time and drift collectively back toward the theater.

"Hail to the king," Merideth muttered.

"What?"

Merideth snapped his clipboard to his side, as if he were a cadet, and watched. "Christopher Hammond, our student director. He's making his appearance. It's a good thing bowing isn't a custom in this country."

Faith turned and knew instantly who Merideth was talking about. Christopher had just parted the aisle curtains and entered the lobby. He wore a loosened tie and a white shirt with the sleeves rolled up. His hair was straight and reddish brown. He seemed to smile at each person in a totally personal way, even if only for a few seconds. Faith guessed that he was a junior or a senior. She couldn't take her eyes off him.

"He's the student director?"

"He's the everything." Merideth held up fingers to count. "Christopher Hammond letters in track. Gets great grades. Majors in communications. Takes theater arts classes because he hopes to get into TV. Does so well in them he was given the small musical to direct. Plus he's a very big muck-a-muck in Omega Delta Tau, some big fraternity."

Suddenly Merideth took his eyes off Christopher and glanced back at Faith. The glance turned into a thoughtful look and then into a smile. "Hey, Ms. I'll-Work-On-Anything, how'd you like to be the assistant director?"

Faith gasped. "What?"

"How'd you like to be Christopher's assistant?"

"But I'm only a freshman."

"Don't move." Merideth deserted her so quickly that Faith froze. When another young man stood next to her, shoulder to shoulder, she barely noticed. Instead she kept watching Merideth, who had caught up with Christopher and was talking in his ear.

Christopher was almost out the door when he paused to listen to Merideth, then spun around to locate Faith. He smiled at her in a way that made her feel she was the most important person in the universe.

"Faith," Merideth called out, "drop off a resume back here by two o'clock tomorrow. Then come on Saturday and Christopher will talk to you about it."

"Really?" Faith whispered in amazement.

A moment later, Christopher, Merideth, and the adoring throngs were gone. Faith was still standing there staring, unable to wipe a goofy smile off her face. "Really?"

That was when she realized that someone was still standing at her shoulder. He moved closer.

"What happened, Faith? Did it work out?"

Faith looked at his face, and for a split second she couldn't figure out who he was.

"Did you get to sign up?" Brooks asked. "I'm sorry I made you late."

It was Brooks. Of course, it was Brooks.

"The list wasn't up." Faith still stared at the open door.

"Maybe it's better that you didn't get to sign

up, anyway. I'm sure they don't let freshmen do anything important."

"Well, this freshman may just get to be the assistant director," Faith objected.

"Really?"

"That guy Merideth just asked me."

"A guy named Merideth?"

Faith saw the doubt on Brooks's face and it suddenly made her doubt too. Something inside her started to crumble. "You're probably right," she said. "Who do I think I am? I'll probably come back on Saturday and they won't even remember me. I'm a fool to take this seriously."

Brooks led the way out of the lobby. "Faith, I never said that."

Faith didn't follow him. She stayed in the theater for another minute or two, until she noticed that Brooks was getting impatient waiting for her out on the stairs.

Six

"If it keeps drizzling like this, I'll melt."

"I'll cry."

"Okay, who smells like a dead horse?"

"Serves me right for wearing angora to the first night of rush."

"Speaking of hoarse, I'm losing my voice."

"I'm sick of smiling. Do I have lipstick on my teeth?"

"No. But you do have a little piece of spinach."

"I don't!"

"You don't. Just kidding."

KC was huddled with Lauren in front of the Tri Beta house. They were in line, eavesdropping on the other potential sorority pledges who stood ahead of them, waiting to be let in for the Tri Beta house tour.

It was the first night of rush, when girls hurried from house to house so they could decide which sororities they liked. The prospective members were checking out the living quarters and the personalities of the sisters, but the sororities were also examining interested girls. There would be more examinations as the week went on, but KC knew the first impression was always the most important.

"Are you warm enough?" KC asked Lauren. The sky was inky dark and it was cold. KC's hair had rebelled into an explosion of frizzy ringlets.

"I'm fine." Lauren shivered.

KC was wearing the black wool dress she'd bought the previous afternoon. She loved it as much as when she'd borrowed Lauren's credit card to pay for it. The dress was simple, expensive, and very grown-up. Unfortunately, it was also knee length and short-sleeved, and the only rain gear KC had was a plastic rain poncho that her mother wore when working in her organic vegetable garden. There was no way KC was going to put it on. She'd only brought it because she had to go to work at The Beanery later that evening. Her teeth were chattering.

Lauren looked only slightly more comfortable in a tan raincoat and tartan scarf. Her lips had a bluish cast and her fluffy hair was deflating. "Does the weather always change so fast out here?" she asked as the line chugged forward and they moved onto the lawn.

"We even have tornadoes sometimes."

Lauren's violet eyes narrowed in alarm.

"This is just plain old drizzly rain," KC assured her. "I wish they'd hurry up."

"It goes so fast once you get inside," Lauren commented.

"I know." KC shuffled her high heels and hugged her goosebumpy arms. "But they sure make you wait before letting you in."

So far that night, KC and Lauren had gone on house tours of five different sororities. At each house they had stood in nervous lines like the one they were currently in while girls were admitted in groups of six. Once inside, however, time sped up. Potential pledges were herded from room to theme-decorated room and looked over, stared at, and sized up in record time.

Tri Beta was the most prestigious and most selective of all the houses. Lauren had been curious about the whole Greek system, and she'd wanted to see other houses, too, saving her mother's alma mater for last. KC had wanted to pay back some of Lauren's generosity, so she'd gone along. But it was getting late, and if the line didn't hurry up, she would never make it to work.

"Thanks again for letting me use your credit card," KC said, rubbing her hands together and realizing that if she got fired from the coffee house she would never be able to pay off the dress. "I promise I'll pay you back as soon as I get paid."

"Don't worry about it," Lauren told her. They moved ahead a few more feet, a little closer to the elegant, warm, dry, important house. "I had a lot better time shopping with you than I do with my mom."

KC rubbed her arms. "Really?"

"She's staying in town this whole week, but I'm trying not to be too dependent on her." Lauren surprised KC by adding, "Going to a store with her is like shopping with Margaret Thatcher."

A joke! It was the first joke KC had heard Lauren make. There was even the tiniest smile on her soft, round face. "I think you dress great."

Lauren seemed pleased with the compliment, as she surveyed the rest of the girls. KC looked over the other hopefuls, too, and felt more and more proud about being linked with Lauren. Dressed in an understated navy-blue crepe shirtdress and pearls, she reminded KC of a museum curator or an English novelist, as opposed to so many of the girls with their plunging necklines and spangles.

"They have to let us in soon," Lauren commented. She seemed to be growing more nervous, chewing on her lip and softly clearing her throat.

The line slithered forward again. KC began to feel anxious, too, but unlike the gigglers around her she merely stood taller, her jaw tighter, her chin held higher.

She and Lauren overheard more rush chatter.

"I heard it just gets more intense as the week goes on," a girl in a strapless satin dress was saying between freezing foot stomps. "My boyfriend told me about one fraternity where they felt they had to accept this pledge, even though they didn't think he was house material. They wanted him to drop out on his own."

"What did they do?"

"They taped him naked to a mattress and put him in front of his girlfriend's dorm."

"Ugh. Sororities don't do things like that, do they?"

"No. Girls are never as horrible as the guys."

"Besides, no one does hazing anymore. It's illegal."

"But all the houses still do things to test you. To make sure you really want to be one of them."

"And to discourage the girls they don't want."

The Tri Beta front door, complete with a brass knocker and a floral wreath, opened up again, swallowing another group of girls. KC and Lauren stepped up to the stoop. KC's heart was beating faster and she clenched her fists to try and calm down. They would be let in with the next set.

Lauren, who had been eavesdropping as intently as KC, turned to her and whispered, "This has been different from what I expected. Some of the other houses were so . . ." She hesitated.

"I know," KC finished for her. "But we won't have to go back to all those houses again. After tonight we can start to narrow down our choices."

"And they can narrow down theirs."

A hopeful pledge broke into scared, uncontrollable giggles. KC cringed. She'd found some of the potential pledges to be true ditz material, not at all what she'd expected from her future business contacts. A few of the sororities had been unappealing, too. Two were blatant party houses, wildly and embarrassingly boy-crazy. There was one egghead sorority, for girls who were studying to be engineers or astronauts. The other houses were fine, attractive, even interesting—but KC thought they were subtly second-rate, back-up sororities so girls had somewhere nice to go when the top houses turned them down.

KC's thoughts were suddenly jolted as the door to Tri Beta swung open and they were invited inside. A rush of warm air floated out, complete with the smell of cider and pine. It lifted KC out of her nervousness and made her think of Christmas.

"Next six girls, please. Be sure to wear your name tags." The young woman at the door had a voice like dark honey and pale blond hair held back with a tortoise-shell headband. Stunning in a classic, Cybill Shepherd way, she wore a red plaid skirt, a little velvet jacket, a blouse with a lace jabot, and patent-leather flats.

KC was so busy staring at her that she almost forget to get rid of the poncho. Quick as lightening, she ducked over to the hedge and tossed it, then made it back in time to follow Lauren and shake hands with the girl at the door.

"I'm Courtney Conner," said the sorority sister, holding out a manicured hand to shake. She took in KC with smart, direct cola brown eyes. "I'm in charge of rush at Tri Beta. Welcome. We hope you enjoy our tour."

KC tried to be discreet as she checked her hand for poncho dirt. She flashed on her family and how everyone always had peat moss or basil or something clinging to their clothes. "Thank you," she managed as she followed Lauren inside.

"Sorry you had to wait in such bad weather," Courtney said. "Please warm yourselves up by the fire."

KC's sense of Christmas had been right on target, since the theme of Tri Beta's open house was "Holiday Seasons." Each house they had visited that night had been elaborately decorated according to a theme, but while some of the other houses had made KC want to smirk, Tri Beta made her want to cry. No dangling crepe paper here. No bowls of punch with suspicious looking foam on top.

The main floor was decorated for the "Holidays of Fall." A fire crackled in a big brick fireplace, surrounded by horns of plenty filled with Indian corn and gourds. There was a Halloween corner, but without rubber masks or tacky witch hats. Instead there were artistically carved jack-o'-lanterns, antique dolls in exotic costumes, and thin slices of pumpkin pie on a long silver tray.

Courtney's eyes seemed to follow Lauren, while other sorority sisters appeared to check out the rest of the girls in the new group. KC was amazed at how much the Tri Betas really looked like sisters. Not that they were all blond or smooth-voiced like Courtney, but every one had Courtney's elegant beauty, her grace, her ease, and her expensive clothes.

"So you're Lauren," Courtney said, planting herself in front of Lauren with clasped hands.

Lauren chewed her lip again and nodded.

"Your mother met our alumni group yesterday," Courtney said. "What do you think they talked about?"

"I don't know."

An awkward moment passed while Courtney waited for Lauren to say something else. "This must be a lot different from back East. Do you think you're going to like it out here?"

"I hope so."

Every house had fired questions at the girls and although Lauren was always shy, at least the other houses had been impressed with her background: prep schools, Switzerland, acceptance to Springfield's prestigious writing program. Lauren, however, wasn't merely quiet this time. She looked like she wanted to run and hide.

"This is my friend, KC," Lauren finally said.

Courtney turned to KC. She seemed confused by Lauren's hesitance, and relieved to turn her social graces elsewhere. Still, when she looked at KC, the bubbly interest in her eyes went flat. KC knew that a house like Tri Beta probably had most of its future members already picked out—girls, like Lauren, whose mothers were Tri Betas. What could the Angelettis donate to the house? Homemade herbed mayonnaise and old Grateful Dead records?

"And what does KC stand for?" Courtney asked.

KC wasn't ready for that one. She had to think fast. "Kind and clever," she responded.

Courtney brought her lovely hands to her mouth and laughed, then looked at KC with new respect. "Well. And what do you plan to study, Kind and Clever?"

Something clicked in KC's brain. She was excited by the situation, and a surge of confidence flooded her. "Undergrad I'm going for a finance degree, and then I'll get my MBA."

Courtney was smiling. "Good. So with your interest in business, what do you think you could contribute to our house?"

KC looked around her, glancing at the expensive food and decorations. "Well, in high school I arranged a benefit concert for our senior class. We raised five hundred dollars in one night."

"Really?"

"I was in charge of booking the groups and settling the contracts. At the last minute two groups canceled out on us and I had two days to find people to fill in. We ended up with the school's jazz combo as the opening act, and I thought I'd have a nervous breakdown, but it all worked out. I love managing, organizing, and problem solving. Anything like that."

"How interesting."

They were interrupted by a high, eerily clear,

singing sound that made KC think of violins or great sopranos. A split second later she realized that it was the ring of a silver spoon being tapped against the side of a crystal goblet.

"Time to switch rooms," a Tri Beta sister announced.

"Very nice to meet you," Courtney told KC as she gestured the girls onward. As an afterthought, she added, "You, too, Lauren. We're glad you decided to rush Tri Beta."

There was no time for further conversation because a moment later they were being led into the "Holidays of Spring" room.

Twenty minutes and three conversations later, KC knew that she should be on her way. She'd stayed at Tri Beta longer than she should have, and she was probably going to be late for work. And the Tri Beta sister in charge of "Holidays of Winter" had already hinted that although she was enjoying her conversation with KC, they had to move on to the next set of prospective pledges.

Still, Beanery or no Beanery, KC refused to budge until she'd heard all of the Tri Beta rush rules. At the other houses she'd barely paid attention to this final speech. But now every syllable out of Courtney's mouth was of utmost importance.

Courtney stood next to a row of decorated

stockings hung on the mantel. Four Tri Betas sat under the Christmas lights, softly singing carols.

"A few final words," Courtney announced over the background of angelic harmony. "Make sure that we have all your schedules and dorm information so you can be found tomorrow. Someone from the Greek organization will give you a list stating which houses would like to invite you back for tomorrow's night of rush. May I remind you that if Tri Beta is on your list, you will be on call. A sister can approach you at any time to check up on you and make sure you are conducting yourself appropriately, or to ask you to do something to help our house. There are certain rules and traditions of rush that you must comply with. On behalf of the whole sisterhood let me say that we enjoyed meeting you all, and we wish you the best of luck."

All the girls seemed to be dawdling, and chattering nervously, as if they knew that most of them would not be invited back and wanted one more moment inside this holiday house. Lauren, however, already had her gloves on and was halfway out the side door.

KC caught up to her. She'd thought she would have been too tired to work four hours after rush, but something about the Tri Beta house had renewed her energy. She was almost skipping, and she knew she'd have no trouble running all the way to The Beanery.

"I have to go straight to work," she told Lauren. Making a quick detour, she grabbed her poncho and shook off little clots of mud.

Lauren nodded, but lingered on the damp sidewalk. KC had the feeling that Lauren might stand there all night.

"What is it, Lauren?"

"They'll never invite me back," Lauren surprised her by stating.

"Don't say that. Of course they'll invite you back. KC didn't want to say, *True, you didn't make much of an impression, but it won't matter because of your connections and your wealth.*

"It's so important to my mother that I get into Tri Beta," Lauren said. "All that pressure kind of made me freeze up. I don't know what I would have done if you hadn't been there."

"You helped me, too. Don't worry. You're exactly the kind of girl they want."

Lauren looked down at herself. "Thanks for saying that."

"It's true. Look, we're in this together," KC promised. "If it weren't for you I wouldn't even be rushing. Lauren, I have to go."

"I know." Lauren clutched her raincoat. "It just means a lot that you're doing this with me."

KC gave her a quick hug.

Before KC could take off, Lauren blurted, "KC, I don't really care that much about the Tri Betas. I'm just glad that we're getting to know each other."

"Me, too." KC dashed across the street. "I really have to go!" she called. "We'll get together tomorrow and wait for the callbacks. Okay?"

"Okay." Lauren began walking slowly back to the dorm.

KC hurried. As soon as she was far enough away from Sorority Row, she unrolled her poncho and let it flap behind her in the cold, damp air.

Seven

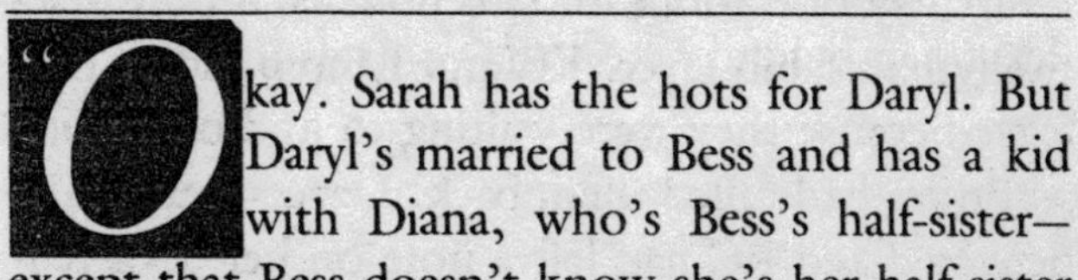

"Okay. Sarah has the hots for Daryl. But Daryl's married to Bess and has a kid with Diana, who's Bess's half-sister—except that Bess doesn't know she's her half-sister because Bess got amnesia after getting hit over the head with a bottle last New Year's Eve—"

"Winnie," KC interrupted, "this is so melodramatic."

"Life is melodramatic, KC. You should hear it in French, though. I'm telling you, dubbed in French even a soap opera comes off like some prizewinning art movie."

"*The Best and the Beloved* was on in France?" asked Faith.

"A lot of American TV is on in Europe," Lauren explained. "It's really popular."

KC scoffed. "Leave it to Winnie to watch a soap opera during her summer abroad. Skip the great museums and go right to *The Best and the Beloved*."

"What's wrong with that?" Faith objected. "I bet it really helped her to learn the language. Didn't it, Winnie?"

Winnie grabbed KC's ankle. "Yes, it did. You're such a snob, KC."

The four of them had been stuck in Faith and Lauren's dorm room for two hours and they practically had cabin fever. KC and Lauren didn't dare leave because they were waiting to find out which sororities had called them back. Letters were being delivered and KC had left a note on her door telling the Sorority Council where they could find her. At the same time, Faith was trying to whip up a quick resume, so she could run it over to the University Theater. And Winnie . . . Winnie was just hanging out.

"See this guy?" Winnie boasted, pointing to an actor on the TV. "That's how sexy the guy I met last night is. He lives right down the hall." She pretended to swoon. "His name's Josh."

"Winnie." Faith lifted her eyes from her typewriter. "Be careful."

"Moi?" Winnie posed dramatically.

Lauren blushed.

"Whatever happened with your roommate?" KC asked Winnie. She paused briefly in front of the mirror, then took a deep breath and looked out the window, past the oak tree that grew right outside.

"She's still the mystery guest," Winnie answered. "By the time I woke up this morning she was already gone. Poof! No jelly beans this time. But she did make her bed."

"Which I'm sure is more than we can say for you," KC reminded her.

"Ha ha." Winnie turned down the sound of the TV as the soap opera faded into a detergent commercial.

"I don't see how you can expect to meet her," KC pointed out, sitting down next to Lauren. "You slept through breakfast."

Winnie told herself not to get defensive. Maybe if she ignored KC's comments, KC would cool out and her little barbs would go away. "True, true," Winnie admitted. "I decided to sleep in. I think we should petition the dining commons to serve breakfast a little later. Like noon." She laughed.

KC ignored her joke.

After a moment of awkward silence, Faith offered a warm chuckle. Lauren tentatively joined in.

"Anyway, I don't think I fell asleep before

three A.M.," Winnie rambled. "I found out last night why they call Forest a party dorm. I think every party hound west of the Rockies moved in. It's a good thing I like heavy metal music."

KC groaned. "You should have worn earplugs."

"What I should have done was gotten up and boogied, too."

Before KC could say anything else, Winnie turned the TV back up.

Faith pushed herself away from her typewriter. She was beginning to get a headache. Her resume, Lauren's anxiety, and the bickering between Winnie and KC were all getting on her nerves.

She watched her friends. KC was edgy. Winnie was trying so hard not to act hurt that she was practically doing cartwheels. And Lauren looked like she wanted to crawl under her bedcovers. Faith wanted to soothe them all, to assure each one that everything would be okay. But she couldn't. She used to be so good at making people feel better, she thought, but that afternoon she didn't know how. She was beginning to get a deep, scary feeling that everything wasn't quite okay inside herself, either.

She took a deep breath. "If none of us has noon classes," she offered, "we should get together and watch this soap opera every day. That way we'd be sure to see each other."

Winnie gave her a grateful look, but KC and Lauren still seemed too nervous and preoccupied to care.

"What are they waiting for?" KC suddenly exploded. She stood up and paced some more. "I wish the Sorority Council would hurry up. I can't stand this much longer."

"Me neither," Lauren breathed.

Faith wasn't sure how KC could take all the sorority nonsense so seriously. But she didn't dare say anything. "Can you guys help me with this resume?" she asked instead. "I have to get it over to the theater before two."

"I'll help you pad it," joked Winnie. "Let's see. 'Won first prize at the Aspen Film Festival with her documentary about a college freshman who met Bigfoot and disappeared forever.' "

Faith stared at the nearly blank page in front of her. Her attempt at a resume hadn't gotten very far. The only words on the page were her name and dorm address.

The morning before, Faith had felt so proud of her accomplishments that she could have reeled them off to Merideth, then and there. But ever since Brooks had hinted that she didn't stand a chance, she felt stuck. Even if she typed up a resume and ran it back over to the University Theater, what then? A big deal like Christopher wouldn't really want some raw, inexperienced freshman for his assistant. Brooks was probably right.

And yet . . .

Last night Faith had started a note to Marlee, but in the middle it had turned into a note to herself.

Faith had written:

To pursue or not pursue assistant directing of Stop the World I Want to Get Off?

Reasons to give up:

Won't get it anyway. Disappointment. Why risk it?

More time for other classes—too soon to take on something so time-consuming.

More time for Brooks.

Who wants a freshman for such an important job? Someone like Christopher Hammond probably has a list five miles long of girls who want to work for him, just to be near his royal presence.

Reasons not to give up:

What if?

That lonely *what if* stuck in Faith's head. *What if* was even scarier than the thought of disappointment and failure. What if she really gave herself to the musical, just threw herself into it? What if she found a whole new part of herself? What if she got totally involved with a bunch of new people and her old friendships started to break down? What if she suddenly didn't want to spend as much time with Brooks! That was the scariest *what if* of all. That *what if* made a knot twist up in Faith's stomach so hard and tight that for a split second she wanted to scream.

Faith couldn't think about *what if* anymore. "KC, how long are you supposed to wait for the sorority callbacks?"

"Good question!" KC burst out. "Maybe I should go back to my own room. What if they can't find me?"

"You said you left a note on your door, KC," Faith said, trying to calm her down.

"I don't know," Winnie goaded, getting up on her knees. "Don't you know what it means to leave a note on your door?"

"What?" KC demanded.

Winnie was practically throwing her words in KC's face. "I found out there's a dorm code on door notes. My neighbor told me that people who want to make their roommate sleep somewhere else on certain nights put a note on their door. An index card with a big Z written on it."

"Why do they do that?" Lauren asked.

Winnie forced a laugh. "Because they're having a guy stay over."

Lauren looked shocked.

"Winnie, I didn't leave a Z card on my door," KC barked.

"You know those uptight sorority girls have so many rules," Winnie prodded. "They may get confused. They just may reject you for immorality."

"Or more likely," KC muttered over her shoulder, "they may reject me for hanging out with you."

Just as Winnie opened her mouth to retort, Faith interrupted. "KC, cool it. And Winnie, you cool it, too."

KC shrugged her shoulders and resumed her pacing. Winnie sat very still. For a moment they could hear the faint bleat of someone practicing scales downstairs and oak leaves brushing against the window.

"I guess I'm nervous," said KC.

"I'll say," grumbled Winnie.

Just then there was a forceful knock on the door. All four heads popped up, staring at the bathrobes hanging on the door hook.

When Lauren didn't budge, Faith got up and opened the door.

A girl was standing there. "Is Lauren Turnbell-

Smythe here?" she asked. She was wearing a sweater dress with a big paisley scarf, and she held a stack of letters and a clipboard. "I'm a representative from the Sorority Council. I'm looking for Lauren and . . ." She stared down at her clipboard, then frowned and stared again. "Is this right? Kind and Clever Angeletti?"

"That's me!" KC cried, practically flying across the room.

The girl checked the name once more, then shrugged and handed a sealed envelope to KC. "Is one of you Lauren?"

Lauren was still motionless, barely breathing. Finally Faith accepted the letter for her. "She is."

The girl said, "Good luck, ladies," then promptly left.

Faith handed the letter to Lauren, who placed it on her lap. At the same time, KC tore open her letter, gawked at it for a few seconds, then leaped up and screamed.

"Waaaheeeee!" she shrieked. *"Yaaaaayaaa!"*

"What does it say?" Faith begged.

"Did Tri Beta ask you back?" Lauren managed.

Even Winnie was interested. "Come on, KC. Tell us."

Coyly, KC pressed the letter against her chest and twirled. But she couldn't hold back for long. She jumped up and down again and hollered, "Tri

Beta asked me back. And so did every single house. *Every single one!*" KC started laughing again, waving her hands and stamping her feet.

"Wait, KC," Faith commanded, "What about you, Lauren?"

"Me?"

"What does your letter say?" Winnie whispered.

Lauren began opening her envelope ever so slowly. Tiny drops of perspiration appeared on her pale brow. She pulled out a sheet of paper but squeezed her eyes shut, refusing to look at it. Faith had to crawl behind her to read it over her shoulder.

"You got called back to Tri Beta, too," Faith blurted, incredibly relieved.

"I did?"

"Look."

Lauren looked down at her short list. There was a long silence. "I did," she finally said. "I guess I did."

Even Winnie joined in as they all cheered and danced and hollered for joy.

Eight

"It's amazing to watch them, isn't it?" said Lauren.

"Amazing is a good word for Barney." Faith giggled. Brooks's roommate, Barney Sharfenburger, had turned out to be a body builder who wore nerdy black glasses and T-shirts so tight they looked painted on. "Winnie calls him half stud, half dud."

Lauren giggled, too, and squinted into the sun. It was several hours after the celebration over the sorority invitations. Winnie and KC had gone off together, and Faith had run errands before meeting Lauren in the late afternoon. They were glad to be outdoors on such a beautiful day, and to be watching Brooks and Barney take part in the latest orientation activity, climbing practice on The Rock.

"C'mon, Brooks, you can do it!" Faith called out.

Brooks waved. The Rock was a huge cement slab formed with cracks and crevices, like the side of a mountain. Surrounded by a sawdust pit, it was a safe place to practice mountain climbing techniques. Brooks wore a rope and a safety harness. Barney was on the ground, holding onto the same rope. If Brooks fell, Barney could take up the slack in the rope to stop the fall.

"Go, Brooks!"

Brooks turned his face ever so slightly, as if making sure Faith was still there, cheering for him. Catching a glimpse of her seemed to give him the extra boost he needed. He went back to his efforts, inching up the concrete wall.

"I have to leave pretty soon to meet my mother again at her hotel," Lauren reminded Faith. As much as she'd been trying to break away from her mother, she'd still seen her every single day. She couldn't wait until classes began and her mother flew back home.

Faith smiled, a little too broadly. "She'll be happy about the Tri Betas, won't she?"

"Yes." Lauren couldn't stop thinking about the sorority list. When she had first looked at it, she was hit with a feeling of doom. She'd been asked back by only three houses. Only three! They included a second-rate house that had asked point-blank how much money her parents made; the egghead house, which had been impressed by her acceptance to the writing program; and the Tri Betas, who would never have asked her back if she hadn't been a legacy. Sure, her mother would be delighted about the Tri Betas, but Lauren knew she still had to make it through several more cuts.

"I wish I could walk over with you," Faith apologized. "Brooks and I are going to the bookstore."

"That's okay." Lauren paused to watch the climbers. "You're lucky to be going to school with Brooks," she said. "It must be great to start college with so many people from home."

"Yes." Faith kept her eyes on Brooks, but her mouth tightened.

Lauren realized that Faith was preoccupied. She also noticed that Faith was wearing Brooks's parka, and had the feeling that Faith would have dressed entirely in Brooks's wardrobe had it been possible.

"Did you get your resume to the theater on time?" Lauren asked.

"No." Faith looked away. "Actually, I decided to forget the whole thing. I'm just a freshman. I won't have time, and they would never pick me anyway." She cleared her throat. "Brooks and I talked about it over lunch. He thinks I should check out the reading lists for the courses I'm going to take, so I know what kind of study load I'm going to be carrying before I sign up for anything extra."

They looked up and saw that Brooks was nearing the top of the concrete incline. Once he got there, he barely paused before tapping the peak and coming back down. All that work and struggling and *whoosh*, as if he were heading down a slide.

But then there was a gasp from the crowd. Faith lurched as Brooks caught his foot and fell. Barney pulled in the slack on his rope, and stopped Brooks's fall, but he couldn't stop him from swinging out and smacking into the rock. Eventually Brooks recovered and controlled the swinging, then Barney carefully used the rope to lower Brooks to the ground.

The crowd gave a collective moan.

Faith took off. She pushed her way through the spectators until she reached Brooks, who was taking off his harness, pulling himself out of the pit and brushing sawdust from his arms and legs. Lauren followed.

"Brooks! Are you okay?" Faith cried.

Brooks made it easily to a nearby bench, where he was joined by Barney. "I'm fine," Brooks said, sounding more angry than hurt. He inspected the mean scrape across his palm.

"Are you sure?" Faith said anxiously. "Let me see your hand. You're bleeding."

"It's just a scratch!" Brooks snapped. He pulled his hand away. "I told you, I'm fine."

Faith stepped back, obviously hurt at being spoken to so harshly. "Okay. Sorry."

Lauren watched the next two climbers step into the pit, a guy in a jumpsuit and a girl in shorts. It was the same girl who'd shared her ice cream with Brooks three days earlier.

Brooks bobbed up and cheered in a strained voice. *"Go for it!"* he yelled, then turned back to Barney. "Let's try again when Greg and Dawn are done."

Barney nodded. "Okay."

"Brooks," Faith suggested, "rest for a while. Don't go up again right away."

Brooks shook his head.

Faith sighed. "Brooks. The bookstore closes at five."

He ignored her.

Faith took a deep breath, then tugged on the neckline of Brooks's T-shirt. "Brooks, I thought you wanted to see how heavy our reading assignments are going to be."

Brooks glanced briefly at the scrape across his palm. "I've got to try one more time."

Faith was starting to show a hint of anger. "Brooks, come on. I have to be back to meet Winnie for dinner. I can tell she's feeling left out by KC so I don't want to desert her. Plus I promised I'd get ready for the toga party tonight in her room. You had a close call. You can try again tomorrow."

Brooks jumped up. "Cheat!" he hollered as Dawn took a running leap at the rock. Brooks made a sound like a game-show buzzer. "Return to go. Do not collect two hundred dollars." He looked down at his palm, then back at Faith. "Let's go to the bookstore tomorrow, all right?"

"Sure, if that's what you want. I just thought you . . ." She shook her head. "Forget it. I'll walk Lauren over to meet her mom. I'll see you tonight at the dance."

Faith and Lauren took off, trudging across campus, over lawns and by buildings. For a long time, neither of them said anything. Lauren hummed, but she stopped when she realized that Faith was kicking at leaves and frowning.

The two girls cut through the athletic facilities. They walked by the stadium and the swimming pool, then around a storage shed and alongside the tennis courts.

"Oh, no," Faith suddenly said, sounding upset and unsure.

"What?" Lauren stopped and looked around. She couldn't see anything that might have startled Faith.

"Nothing. Let's keep going," Faith said quickly.

"Just a second, Faith. I have to—"

A tennis ball smacked against the metal fence, and a male voice yelled, "My set!"

Lauren realized that two guys had been in the middle of a match and that one was jogging across the court to fetch the stray ball. The player scooped up the ball, but instead of heading back to the court, he stared at them.

"Don't I know you?" he asked, looking first at Lauren, then at Faith, and back again.

Lauren's lips parted, but no sound came out. He looked like a junior or a senior. Even though he was wearing shorts and a polo shirt, with a sweatband around his wrist, there was something about him that almost made it seem as if he were dressed in a tuxedo.

"I know you, I'm sure of it," he repeated.

Lauren could barely speak. She usually had trouble with ordinary social conversations, but this was like asking her to sing opera under water.

Then she heard Faith's voice. She sounded a little defensive. "Yes. I was at the auditions yesterday," she admitted.

Lauren jammed her hands in the pockets of her skirt and turned away so no one would see her blush. Of course the tennis player hadn't been talking to her. It was Faith he'd recognized.

The guy was leaning against the fence now, looking hard at Faith. "I'm sorry, but I can't remember your audition."

"Well, that's because I didn't audition." Faith was flustered, too. Lauren had never seen her so off-balance. Faith's fingers gripped the cuffs of Brooks's jacket.

The other tennis player joined them. He was about the same age as his friend, but had short dark hair and a mustache. He wore gym shorts and a U of S sweatshirt. When he reached the fence, he leaned on it, crossing his arms. He didn't have the sparkly charm of his tennis partner. In fact, he was looking Faith and Lauren up and down as if they were for sale.

"Why didn't you audition?" asked the first guy. "You have the perfect look for one of the daughters–innocent, fresh."

His friend continued to leer.

Faith explained. "I'm not a performer."

"Oh, wait," he said, breaking into a dimpled, paper-white smile that lit up his whole face. His intelligent eyes twinkled. "You were the one Merideth mentioned just as I was leaving. He said you might want to be my assistant. Faith, right? Your name stuck in my head."

"Yes."

"I'm Christopher Hammond," he said, acknowledging Lauren now.

Christopher, the director. Faith had mentioned that he was a big wig, but Lauren had never imagined this. He had an air of assurance, as if he owned the planet but was kind enough to allow everyone else to live there. "Hi. I'm Lauren Turnbell-Smythe," she managed in a barely audible whisper.

Christopher stuck out a hand to shake, then made a joke of not being able to fit it through the fence. He observed Lauren's expensive clothes, but not with his friend's hungry wolf eyes. Christopher looked Lauren over with big-brotherly affection. "You must be rushing."

Lauren nodded.

"How's it going? Being a rushee can be tough. It was a few years ago for me, but I'll never forget."

"She got called back by the Tri Betas," Faith offered.

Christopher looked impressed. "Good for you."

The guy with the mustache spoke up. "I'm Mark Geisslinger. I'm Chris's roommate at ODT."

"That's a fraternity," Lauren whispered to Faith.

"Omega Delta Tau. *The* fraternity," Mark teased, having overheard her. "Chris is on the Interfraternity Council."

"I'll put in a good word for you with a friend at Tri Beta," Christopher said. He smiled right at Lauren, and she felt something inside glimmer like a campfire. "As for you," he said, turning back to Faith, "I could sure use an assistant director who's smart and enthusiastic."

"Well," Faith hedged, "I didn't drop off my resume like Merideth asked me to. I mean, I tried to, but other things came up."

Christopher waved a hand. "I didn't have time to go over to the theater today, either. Just drop it by sometime this week."

Christopher continued to smile at Faith, but she suddenly turned away and said, "I have to get back to the dorms."

Mark lingered at the fence a moment longer. "Good luck with rush," he said to Lauren.

"Thank you."

Mark winked. "Maybe I'll see you at our house party tomorrow night."

The two guys picked up their gear and left the court, Mark racing and jumping to swipe at leaves with his racket and Christopher running with steady and purebred grace. They turned onto Fraternity Row and disappeared.

Faith and Lauren stood quietly for a moment, overwhelmed. When they met each other's eyes again, they both grinned.

The grins turned to laughter.

"Wow," Lauren squeaked. "That guy, Christopher, is really something."

"Tell me about it!"

"Faith!"

They laughed so hard that tears started to run down Lauren's cheeks. She thought about her mascara running and realized that a Tri Beta could very well jump out of the bushes to admonish her, but she didn't care. She hadn't enjoyed silly, friendly giggling like this very often. And besides, she couldn't have stopped herself, even if she'd wanted to.

Nine

"Winnie, are you sure that's how it works?"

Winnie tugged on one end of her dorm-issued bedsheet, and yanked it off the mattress. "Of course, Faith! I'm always sure. Of everything." She twisted the sheet around herself and posed. "Toga by Winnie!"

"I should have known you'd be an expert in togas," said Faith.

"At least I'm an expert in something." Winnie pulled down the straps of her bra and tried to tuck them in her armpits. Then she began retucking and draping while staring at herself in her mirror. No matter what she did with her bra straps they still stuck out, so she finally pulled off her bra and whirled it around her head while Faith whistled and made cat calls. Winnie hammed it up, then tossed her bra past the mess of dirty clothes that surrounded her bed.

It landed in her absent roommate's wastebasket.

"Two points," KC announced. She was sitting at Melissa's desk. In front of her was a stack of red construction paper from which she was cutting small hearts. She fished the bra out of the wastebasket. "Winnie, where should I put this?"

Winnie was still twisting, pinning, and redraping her toga.

"Wherever."

KC tossed the bra back on Winnie's bed. "There. It's on your side of the room." KC tried to hold back a huge yawn, then gave in to it. "At least I think it's on your side of the room. In this mess, it's hard to tell."

"It's not a mess. It's decor." Winnie had taped European postcards, photos, and clippings from magazines all over the walls. There were male models, and phrases taken out of context, including two newspaper headlines, "Gottlieb's Extraordinary Exhibition" and "Free Winnie."

KC glanced around at the hills and dales of clothes, towels, makeup, raisin boxes, and dumbbells. She yawned again.

"KC, you sure look tired," Winnie said. "Maybe you should wear a toga to the rush party tonight. Then if you fall asleep, you'll already have your bedding with you."

"Very funny."

"Hey, maybe you could make togas a new rush ritual. I've been hearing how you have to learn secret handshakes and sorority songs." Winnie snorted. "There's one sorority that's making the rushees walk around with rice in their shoes. Sick."

"Winnie," Faith soothed.

"You don't understand." KC yawned again as a thundering bass line boomed from a stereo downstairs. A moment later a rock vocal megablasted, followed by the horrendous screech of a needle being dragged across an LP. More sounds followed: laughter, yells, and the clunk of furniture being moved.

KC stopped cutting. "I guess the wild and crazy Forest residents have officially arrived."

"Yeah," Winnie cracked. "Spuds McKenzie lives right down the hall."

KC laughed.

"At least, you appreciate my jokes again," Winnie commented.

"We always appreciate your jokes, Winnie," Faith assured her.

KC went back to her paper hearts, saying nothing.

Winnie tried to stay cool. She'd been stewing over her friendship with KC all afternoon. With Faith and Lauren off watching Brooks climb The Rock, Winnie had asked KC to come over. She wanted to talk and forgive, so they could start over and get silly the way they used to. She needed to tell KC the truth about her summer. She needed to know that KC and she would continue being friends.

But a Tri Beta had magically appeared and ordered KC to cut out a hundred red hearts for that evening's social event. Winnie was sure that KC would say, "I can't. I have plans with my old friend"–but she hadn't. KC had instantly forgotten about Winnie and started to work, as if she loved the idea of being a sorority slave.

So Winnie had made a decision. If KC wasn't going to be there for her the way she used to, other people would fill in. Like her mother said, she had to take off, spread her wings, and fly. Forget KC! Winnie would just take a bigger leap–into everything.

Winnie modeled her toga, but KC was concentrating on the hearts. Faith was slowly wandering around the room, picking up Winnie's dirty clothes.

Winnie hopped in front of Faith. "All right. Your turn now."

"For what?" Faith asked, looking up and sweeping back her long hair, which for once flowed freely down her back.

Rubbing her hands together, Winnie threw back her head. "A toga. You're the only other one going to the party."

Faith put her hands to her face and backed toward the door. "No! Besides, I don't have a sheet. I don't want to go all the way back to my dorm. I'll just go like this," Faith explained, gesturing to her work shirt and form-fitting jeans.

"It's a toga party, Faith. Not a rodeo rider's convention."

Faith was half giggling, half frowning. As Winnie approached she flapped her hands as if she and Winnie were going to box. "I have to meet Brooks soon. Really, Win. Besides, I can't wear your bottom sheet. The elastic would look dumb."

Faith reached for the doorknob, but Winnie got there first and blocked the exit. "That's the whole point. Come on, Faith, loosen up. Wear a toga."

"I don't think so."

"Toga time."

"I'm not the toga type."

"We'll see what we can do about that." Winnie was already shoving aside her absent roommate's quilt and whipping the top sheet off Melissa's bed. "That's the beauty of this whole operation," she said, flinging the sheet with a snap. "One size fits all." Winnie swung Faith around in front of her and began to tuck and fold the sheet over her clothes.

Faith started to get into it. She inched closer to the mirror. "What do you think?" she asked, daring to look.

Winnie stepped back and looked at her work. Then she said, "Your clothes. They've got to go."

Faith put her hands to her face and shrieked. "You can't expect me to go naked to this thing!"

"You're not going naked, you'll be wearing a toga!" Winnie said as she poked at Faith's shirt. "Come on, Faith."

"But what will Brooks say?"

"He'll love it!" Winnie cried.

Soon Faith was wrapped in almost nothing but Melissa's sheet. Winnie began doing an interpretive dance around the room, tossing TV guides and paperback books. Faith followed her. They minced and did little leaps, made silly arm gestures, skipped and twirled.

Winnie was getting so caught up, she might have danced into the hall if KC's voice hadn't interrupted harshly. "Winnie, what about your roommate?"

The dance stopped.

"What about her?"

"You can't take her sheet."

Something inside Winnie threatened to snap. If she heard one more word of criticism from KC, she thought, she was going to shoot through the roof. And she didn't want to think about her invisible roommate, who was just one more person who wasn't there when Winnie needed her.

"She has a bottom sheet," Winnie retorted, throwing herself into her dance again. "Fashion is born of sacrifice."

"But it's not your sheet."

Winnie clenched her fists. "KC, since when did you turn into Ms. Fair Play? What is with you lately, anyway?"

"What's with *you*?" KC shot back.

"Nothing is with me. Believe me, I'm the same old Winnie."

Faith quickly came between them. "Come on, you guys. We're all the same as we've always been. It's just everything else that's different."

For a moment all three of them were silent, as the stereo downstairs shook the walls and bellowed through the floor. They didn't look at one another.

KC packed up her paper hearts. "Lauren should be back from dinner with her mom, soon," she said, heading for the door. "I said I'd pick her up over at Coleridge. Have a good time in your togas."

Without another word or look or smile, KC was gone.

Winnie just stood there for a while, staring after KC and feeling empty. Even the music downstairs stopped temporarily. It was as if everyone in Forest had decided to retreat to their rooms for a quiet rest at exactly the same time.

"You know, Win, KC is right," Faith said, slowly unwrapping her toga. "I can't take Melissa's sheet."

"Why not?" Winnie screamed, stamping her foot. "For all I know, Melissa doesn't even exist! I've certainly never seen her. In the daylight, that is. Keep the sheet."

Faith shrugged. "Okay."

"Come on." Winnie grabbed Faith's bare arm, dodged a stereo speaker, her pair of Heavy Hands, and a pile of socks, and led Faith to the doorway. The coast was clear.

"WOULD EVERYONE STOP WORRYING ABOUT EVERYTHING FOR ONCE!" Winnie ranted, her voice blasting down the empty hall.

A moment later she was answered by a pair of male voices.

"All right!"

"What, me worry?"

Winnie took off in a run, dragging Faith behind her. Josh's door was closed, but across the hall a bunch of guys were sitting in an open room, drinking beer. They had just put on a record. When they looked up and saw Faith and Winnie they all broke into a chant.

"To-*ga*! To-*ga*! To-*ga*!"

The Tri Beta house was lit up like an ornamented Christmas tree. Above it stars were popping out. In front, clusters of girls chattered in the moonlight.

Despite her fight with Winnie, KC felt excited and happy. "Do I look okay?" she asked Lauren. She was wearing a cashmere sweater of Lauren's over the black pleated skirt she'd bought for her senior awards night.

Lauren gazed at her with open envy. "You look beautiful."

"Thanks."

KC felt she was on the right track, in spite of the way Winnie kept needling her about rushing Tri Beta. Sure, KC felt weird about how she'd been treating Winnie, and she knew that it might damage their friendship. But just then she had to concentrate on other things.

KC yawned. She was tired, as Winnie said she was. Who wouldn't be tired after attending Tri Beta's open house the night before, then waitressing until two and getting up at six that morning to make sure she had an hour to get dressed—really dressed, in case a Tri Beta popped out of the bushes to check up on her? Plus she'd spent a couple of hours buying some of her books and had still managed to go to the study workshop and make one hundred heart-shaped doilies.

"I decided to rush *only* Tri Beta," KC told Lauren. "I've been talking to girls today, trying to find out everything I can about all the sororities. Tri Beta is by far the top house. What about you?"

"I guess I could do that, too," Lauren said. "That's what my mother wants."

"I know I should have a second choice to fall back on," KC explained. "If I don't, it's either Tri Beta or nothing. They call it suiciding. But I want to take the chance."

Lauren winced. "Okay. I'll risk it if you will."

KC had also realized that it would be impossible to attend all the house parties, to do favors for all the sisters, and still give Tri Beta one hundred percent. Not to mention working at The Beanery. But it was more than that.

"The Tri Betas have the most tradition. The most class," KC added. "They have formal teas and sit-down dinners. Even those paper hearts I made are part of some rush tradition for tonight. I guess rush has lots of rituals. Like the dream date party, which is tomorrow night."

Lauren stared off at the wide, dark sky. "The what?"

"The dream date dance." KC looked around at the other girls collecting in front of the house. She was mentally scoring each girl on the basis of clothes, face, figure, and attitude, and wondered how her own total would stack up against theirs. "A frat guy asks a rushee to be the date for another guy in his house. The guy asks the girl he thinks his frat brother would most want to go out with. That's why they call it a dream date."

"How did you find all this out?"

"I've been doing my homework." KC smiled and went on. "Now, the girl doesn't know who her dream date is. The frat guy who sets the date up just presents the dream date girl with a playing card. Then when she gets to the dance, the guy with the identical card is her date."

Lauren hugged her arms. "It sounds romantic."

KC hadn't thought of it that way. She'd never had an all-consuming romance; she sometimes suspected that falling in love was overrated.

Men's voices were suddenly audible, singing old songs in four-part harmony. A series of fraternity choirs began to stroll by, led by a black fraternity group singing the school's alma mater. All the guys were in sport coats and striped ties, with neat haircuts and shoes that shined under the streetlights as they strolled from house to sorority house. Most of them stopped for the longest time in front of Tri Beta.

"Listen to that," KC sighed after one choir held a long, low note and finally strolled on to the next house. "Compared to all the boring guys I knew in high school, this could make you want to wake up and start dating."

Lauren watched the boys stroll by. Serenading seemed to be another rush tradition, and the voices were musical and cheery. Being face to face with Christopher Hammond that day had given her a jolt. And the thought of having to go through three more cuts, three more nights of imagining herself as the victim of cold, cruel discussion at the post-party sessions they called "hash," practically made Lauren's brain waves go flat. Still, she followed KC and the other girls out of the mountain breeze and into the perfumed living room of the sorority mansion.

The whole first floor of the Tri Beta house had been redecorated. Lauren had no idea how it had been redone so quickly, especially since the new decor was just as impeccable as before. One holiday, Valentine's Day, had been picked for this reception. The whole living room was done in pinks and violets, with lacy doilies everywhere.

As the girls squeezed onto sofas and chairs, Courtney Conner, dressed this time in a red smock dress with a white crocheted collar, made her way to the blazing fireplace. As she passed KC and Lauren, she smiled.

"Welcome to our party, ladies," Courtney began in her smooth, liquid voice. "We'll get started now, since I know some of you have other house parties to attend." She stopped to give the group a coy wink. "Although I also suspect that you've all figured out that this house is number one."

Nervous titters.

"First, I would like to congratulate you on being called back," Courtney continued. "We were impressed with each and every one of you and hope that you feel the same way about us. Tonight you will each have a one-to-one chat with a Tri Beta sister, so that we can get to know you better and figure which of you will really be suited to our house." Another sister walked up to Courtney with a silver platter of what looked like valentines, the red hearts that KC had cut out that afternoon.

Courtney held up one valentine as the other sister passed the rest around the living room. "We would like you each to take a Valentine," Courtney instructed. "On the inside you will find the name of a girl in our sisterhood. That is the girl you will have your chat with tonight."

KC opened her valentine while Lauren dawdled, fiddling with the folded paper until she could delay it no longer. While other girls were already waving hands in the air and matching their hearts with a sorority sister, she was still playing with the paper, as if she weren't sure what to do with it.

When Lauren looked up again, most rushees were paired up with a sister and were already taking off to some prearranged location. Lauren finally opened her note, but it was too late. Her chat partner had already found her.

"You must be my rushee," the sister said, looking down. She had a slight drawl and sounded like she was from Texas or Louisiana.

Lauren read the name on her heart. "Marielle Danner?"

"That's me."

Marielle wore a backless dress and three chunky charm bracelets that clinked loudly. Her hair was parted on the side and kept falling over one eye, despite her habit of constantly flicking it back. She had a tiny nose and perfect teeth, and was very thin. "Follow me up to my room—" She paused to check Lauren's name tag, which was also heart-shaped. "—Lauren."

Lauren trailed Marielle up the stairs. She wanted

to connect with KC for moral support, but KC was standing with a sister in front of the French doors, laughing.

Marielle's room was on the second floor. On her desk was a computer and ceramic jars containing make up brushes and pens. Photos of Marielle and her roommates with great-looking guys were all over the walls.

Marielle picked up the alarm clock and set it on the bed next to her. "I have to stay on schedule. We're still seeing a lot of girls."

"Of course."

Marielle settled herself on the bedspread. "So Lauren," she began, looking Lauren over from head to toe, "tell me, if you could have any holiday last all year, which would it be?"

"Holiday?" Lauren's head was a blank. When she sat alone at her computer, words came to her in rushes. Phrases flooded her mind at night, keeping her awake and forcing her to keep a notebook next to her bed so that she could jot ideas down. But face to face with Marielle, she had almost nothing to say. "New Year's Eve."

"Why?"

"Well, um, because you get to start another year all over."

"Okay." Marielle pursed her mouth. "If you were a color, which would you be?"

Lauren looked around the room and her eyes settled on a poster of Sting over one of the single beds. Sting was wearing a gray felt hat. "Gray."

Marielle's tiny nose wrinkled. "If someone gave you a million dollars, what's the first thing you'd buy?"

Fantasizing about money was something Lauren had never had to do. Actually, she sometimes thought things would be easier for her if her parents hadn't been so rich. "I don't know."

"Do you have a boyfriend?"

Lauren shook her head.

"What do you like to do for fun?"

"Read, I guess."

Marielle looked down at her clock. For a moment she fiddled with her charm bracelets, fingering a golden dog and a little gold badminton racket. "Look, Lauren, I'll be brutally honest," she said. "It's kind of a weird coincidence that you drew my heart, because I dinged you."

"You what?"

"I was *going* to ding you, I mean. Vote against having you come back. Courtney talked me out of it."

Lauren felt her heart practically stop.

Marielle touched the corners of her mouth, as if she had just eaten something slightly messy. "I just want you to know that you may be in over your head here. And if you really want to make it into this house, you'll have to try a little harder."

She checked her clock. "Time's up. I wish you all the luck in the world."

"Thank you," Lauren whispered on her way back down the stairs.

The next group of callbacks was already gathering in the living room. Lauren thought of hightailing it down to the other two houses that had asked her back. She realized that the egghead house might be a good place for her. But before Lauren could take a step toward the door, KC rushed up to meet her.

"Lauren, how did it go?"

"Oh, fine."

KC was breathless and flushed. "They asked which holiday I wanted to last all year and I said February twenty-ninth. Not that it's even a holiday, but I said it would be this magical day where we would get to do four years' worth of things that would get us ahead of everyone else. I don't think I even made sense, but Joelle—that was my sister—laughed and laughed." KC caught her breath and took Lauren's hands. "I love this house. It was the right decision, to rush only Tri Beta. Don't you think so, too?"

Lauren tried not to tremble. "Oh, yes. I think so. I think so, too."

Ten

"I think somebody broke the springs on this couch."

Back inside the lobby of Forest Hall, Winnie was sitting on the armrest of a sofa, smiling at another freshman. She hadn't actually tried the cushions, but she could believe the couch was broken. Ten or eleven people at a time had been lumped together on it. Apart from the bandstand near the fireplace, the sofa was the one island in a sea of writhing, dancing, yakking, and partying dorm freshmen. It wasn't exactly a calm island, either. The couple on the far end was making out wildly. Three boys had shaken up a can of soda and sprayed a girl sitting in the middle. Another couple had decided that one of the cushions could be used for a nifty pillow fight. Winnie decided that they should get the award for most novel way to get to know each another.

But Winnie wasn't getting to know anybody. She was perched on the armrest in her toga, feeling like the figurehead on the prow of a ship. All around her the raucous, foot-stomping atmosphere made it easy for people to talk and dance with total strangers. But she just sat there, watching everything swirl past.

She tried to keep up a smile, but wasn't about to throw herself into the party. At first she'd put it down to still fretting about KC, or feeling guilty over stealing Melissa's sheet. Every time she looked at Faith in her toga, she almost felt like crying.

Of course, Winnie hadn't seen Faith for the last half-hour. Faith had gone outside on the lawn to dance with Brooks. She was probably acting a little more placid and controlled than the other party-goers, but having a great time nonetheless. Winnie envied Faith. No matter how hard Winnie tried to give the impression of being a wild, out-of-control party beast, she really liked the idea of being with some guy who was nice, and safe—a trusted high school sweetheart and very best friend.

Which made her wonder about Josh. Not that Josh could ever be those things—or could he? Besides, Winnie hadn't even seen him at the party yet. At least she didn't think she had. There were so many freshmen, and the assault on her senses was so complete, that it was hard adjusting to the music and the loud talking and the dozens and dozens of togas.

"Hello, there," said a boy who had just sat down on the couch next to her. He spun the long end of his toga around his finger like a ladies fur. He looked a little out of it, with red eyes and hair sticking straight up in a punked-out crew cut.

Winnie smiled. "Hi."

"I'm Kirk. As in Captain." He laughed at his own joke. "Having a good time?"

"Great," Winnie came back, much too quickly.

"You live in Forest?"

Winnie nodded.

"Me, too," Kirk said. "Great dorm."

Winnie was trying to think of something to keep the conversation going when Kirk turned away from her and reached for an object stowed between his knee and the couch cushion. The two guys next to him—the ones who had been showering the girl with soda fizz—watched, smirking as if they had a secret. When the guy sat up again, he held a bottle. Paper cups appeared in the hands of each of his pals.

"Juice of the Starship Enterprise," Kirk said,

grinning at the liquor bottle. He gave the party a once-over again, then leaned over to his buddies and began to pour. He handed Winnie a cup, then hesitated. "Do you like rum?" He nudged her with his shoulder and held the bottle up near her chin.

Winnie had never tasted rum. Once over the summer she had drunk too much red wine and had pretty mixed memories of that. When Kirk pushed the neck of the bottle in her face, the odor of something sweet and sharp stung the inside of her nose.

Kirk laughed. "I don't want to corrupt anybody."

"It's a little late for that," Winnie boasted. "I drank wine all summer when I was in . . ." Winnie let her voice peter out, since he obviously wasn't listening. She didn't get to tell him that her mother had a relaxed attitude about drinking, and had even said that if Winnie wanted to experiment with alcohol, she could do it at home.

Kirk was checking for RAs again, then turned and pulled Winnie down onto his lap.

"To-*ga*, to-*ga*," Kirk's buddies chanted.

"This girl needs to loosen up," Kirk slurred.

"I'm loose."

He started laughing hysterically and tipped the cup up to Winnie's mouth. "Did you hear, guys? This girl is loose."

Winnie thought the guys were obnoxious, but she was the last person who wanted to be accused of being uptight or a prude. And besides, was she going to take the leap or wasn't she? Was she going to get a reputation as a dud or as a girl with experience and sex appeal? She took the drink and knocked it back as if it were milk.

"Oh, my God," Winnie spluttered as she choked. The rum hit the back of her throat like fire. It clawed at her sinuses. Her eyes watered and she began to cough uncontrollably.

Kirk and his buddies broke into applause.

"Yes, mama!"

"This girl has hair on her chest."

"To-*ga*, to-*ga*."

Winnie lifted herself off Kirk's lap. The cough was gone and the burning wasn't quite so painful. Just when she was beginning to wonder if she'd done something really dumb, a warmth started in her middle and spread through her arms and legs. It felt like hot light was swirling around her body, making her worries about KC and mysterious Melissa fade away and causing her screwups and her summer abroad to fade further and further into the distance, too. Winnie started to laugh, and the sound flowed out like fast, warm water.

"Shall we have another?" Kirk winked.

Up came the paper cups. Kirk poured again.

"Cheers."

All at the same time, Winnie and the boys guzzled.

The rum went down more easily the second time. The burning had shifted to Winnie's chest, just under her collarbone, but the pleasant warmth was getting stronger. And her insides were starting to bubble. No longer stiff and wooden, she felt giddy. Her face was hot, and she was glad to be wearing only a draped cotton sheet.

The music seemed even louder now. By the time that Winnie had finished her third cup of rum, the lobby was alive. Couples were bouncing around like pogo sticks, and there was a shimmer to the lights. Winnie finally decided that she was going to throw off all her doubt and just dance. She didn't have a partner, but even if she couldn't find one on the dance floor, nobody would notice the difference.

She managed to stand up. Kirk tried to follow her, but his friend pulled him back down. A moment later they were drinking again, and Winnie was on her own.

Dancing by herself, Winnie plunged into the crowd's center. It was like being rolled around in human Play-Doh. It was warm and squishy and fast and violent all at the same time. The music went right to the bone. Winnie felt the sweat zip down her back and the rum in her senses, and forgot about everything. For once she wasn't going to be her self-judging, self-stopping, self-conscious self—to borrow all the terms she'd learned from her mother. She was just going to be one cell in the big, living organism that was her first freshman dorm dance.

Out on the lawn, Brooks noticed Faith craning her neck.

"Who are you looking for?" he asked, as they moved to the beat. The music was muted out there. The freshmen weren't shoved together. The dark sky went on forever, and the air was breezy and cool. But despite all that freedom and space, Faith's dancing felt constrained.

"Just Winnie."

"Oh. I saw her when I was inside a little while ago."

"Was she having a good time?"

"She was dancing like a maniac. Don't worry about Winnie."

"Okay."

Brooks pulled Faith closer. "Faith, don't worry about anything."

Her dancing became even stiffer.

For one of the first times in their long relationship, Brooks didn't know what else to say. He dipped Faith in a corny tango move, which made her smile, but a moment later she seemed far away again. Even dancing slowly, intimately, with her bare, tanned shoulders slipping out from the edge of her toga, Faith felt strangely distant to him.

When the song ended they stepped apart, as if they'd never danced before.

"It's beautiful out here," Faith finally said.

"It sure is." A breeze came up as they waited for the next song. "You warm enough?"

"Of course I'm warm enough." Faith frowned.

Faith's muted anger was unfamiliar, too. Since he'd made the mistake about directions to the theater, he'd seen a new, pent up look in her eyes. "Faith, I just asked because you're wearing a toga and it's not all that warm out here. It's a reasonable question."

"I know. I just . . . never mind."

"What?" The music had started again, but Brooks stood stock-still. "Do you think I should have worn a toga, too? Is that it? I mean, you look great, but it's not in the freshman rule book that we all have to throw ourselves into every dumb thing on campus."

"Brooks, I don't care whether or not you wear a toga." Faith sighed. "You just don't always have to worry about whether I'm cold or I'm okay or I'm safe. That's all."

"Sorry."

They started dancing again, but Brooks was feeling totally out of sync. He wasn't sure how things between him and Faith had gotten so testy. Sure, he'd been a jerk earlier that day at the climbing rock. But who wouldn't have been after banging against the rock like that? He wished that Faith hadn't been there to see. And, yes, he was worried he wouldn't be able to handle Honors College. But those were *his* problems, not Faith's. It was his job to take care of her, not the other way around.

"You know, it's been a while since we danced, hasn't it?" He pressed his cheek against hers. He wanted things to be the way they had been before: simple, effortless, and secure.

"I think the last time we danced was the senior prom."

Brooks remembered the prom and held Faith more tightly. "You looked so great that night. I'll never forget when you walked into your living room wearing that white dress." He laughed. "I was trying to act so together and responsible in front of your dad, and the whole time I thought I was going to start drooling on the carpet."

He felt her soften. Faith pulled back to look into his face. "You never told me that."

Brooks was a little embarrassed. "I don't tell you everything."

"Why not?" The question surprised him, and he couldn't think of an answer.

Faith looked into his eyes a little longer, then rested her head against his arm. "Never mind. I guess I don't tell you everything either."

They danced again, but it was all wrong. Brooks felt as if they were just two bodies with nothing in common, barely moving to the same beat.

"Brooks, is there something you wanted to talk about?" she suddenly asked.

Brooks was off guard. He had a lot on his mind, but nothing he wanted to worry her with. "I guess I was thinking how lucky we are."

"Are we?"

"Of course." He pulled her closer. "Before this party, everybody in my dorm seemed so nervous, so desperate to have a good time and meet somebody. Like Barney. He was so nervous he retied his toga about a dozen times."

Faith laughed. "Winnie was nervous, too."

"But we don't have to go through all that."

"We don't?"

Brooks slid both arms around Faith's waist and danced so slowly he barely moved. He just wanted to take in the feel of her skin and the smell of her silky hair. "Because we've already found each other. I've been realizing that tonight. It's great to get to know new people and all—"

"It is."

"—but it's also great to be with the same person for a long time."

Faith put her arms around his neck. "I know." There was a little catch in her voice.

Brooks stopped moving. He leaned his forehead against Faith's and for a while they stood like that. Then he lifted her chin and gave her a long, sweet kiss, exactly like a hundred other long, sweet kisses he had given her a hundred other times.

Winnie had been jumping and flailing for forty-five minutes. She was just beginning to loosen up and forget all the things she wanted to forget and flow with the music. Then she felt a tap on her shoulder.

"Hey, Winnie."

"Josh?"

Josh had spotted her amid all the bodies and shouldered his way over. His toga revealed a swimmer's chest and smooth skin. He had a plastic pocket protector clipped to the top of his toga, but even that computer nerd joke only made him more attractive.

"Where have you been? I've been looking for you all night. I was beginning to think I wouldn't see you," Winnie blurted. The minute she said it, she wondered if she'd come on too strong. The rum had shortened the space between her thoughts and her mouth, a space that had never been too big to begin with.

"Good to see you, too. Wild party, huh?"

"What?"

"Wild party," Josh shouted.

"What?" Winnie yelled, still unable to hear him.

Josh said something else, but Winnie only saw his mouth move. They were standing in the middle of the moving mass, getting elbowed and stepped on and shoved from side to side. A girl whose toga was drooping dangerously low wiggled between them until a guy scooped her up by her hips and threw her over his shoulder.

"Let's dance!" said Winnie.

Josh started moving to the music. He didn't take dancing very seriously, but hopped around, shaking and jiggling with abandon. Winnie let go. She waved her arms and swung her hips, throwing her body around and reaching out to Josh.

The band finished the number and went into a slow tune. Josh just stood there, but that didn't faze Winnie. She had a new alcohol-fueled courage. New, loose, warm-limbed courage. She stepped right up to him, took his arm and pressed it around her waist, then leaned her body against his. He wrapped his arms around her and they swayed and stepped to the music.

When the slow song ended and the band punched into a fast song again, Josh looked around with a funny smile. Winnie led him away, back to the sofa, which Kirk and his buddies had vacated. The couple making out were still at it, and the pillow-fight pair had gotten the same idea. Winnie was still flying. When Josh planted himself on the armrest, she dropped down onto his lap. And then she did something she'd wanted to do ever since they'd met.

She kissed him.

It was a strange kiss. A sort of out-of-the-body kiss, as if her mind were saying, *This is what you are supposed to do.* But at the same time her mouth didn't quite feel the softness of Josh's lips, even though she was right against him. She was trying too hard. Her hand was on his bare shoulder, and she didn't feel the silkiness of his skin. For a split second his arms hung at his sides, as if he couldn't believe that she had really kissed him. But then, just when Winnie began to feel another rush of doubt, he pressed in closer to her, and put one hand along her cheek, the other behind her back.

A moment later he pulled back and looked into her eyes. They sat there like that, still and close, until the end of the next song.

"Hi," he said when the music died down.

"Hi," Winnie breathed in return.

This was a new kind of warmth for Winnie. It felt peaceful and sweet, and flowed slowly through every inch of her. It made her want to weep.

"You okay?" he asked.

"Great. The best," she said instantly, trying to push down the swell of feeling he provoked in her. She feared that she really might start to cry, so she giggled instead. "I guess I feel a little weird. I kind of had a lot to drink. Rum."

He brushed a stray, damp hair away from her forehead. "I figured it was something like that."

He looked into her eyes again with a seriousness that made her self-conscious. She took his hand, which was warm and dry and made her aware that her own palms had become clammy. A moment later the dancers were at it again and the whole room was swirling. Her dizziness was getting worse, and she flopped against Josh.

He stood up and helped her to her feet. "Maybe we should get some air."

Winnie's thoughts were blurry, but something was coming through loud and clear. It told her that she hadn't gone far enough yet, that she hadn't taken any kind of real leap.

"We could go to my room," she said.

Josh just looked at her.

She giggled. "Oh, wait. I forgot. My roommate

might be there and I stole her sheet. But if she's not there, we could put a Z card on the door."

Josh looked puzzled.

Winnie tugged at her toga, which was twisted around her legs. "You know, a Z card?" she repeated. "Oh, never mind."

Something in the back of her mind tried to tell her she was in dangerous waters, but her knees were shaky and she was starting to feel so warm. She held onto Josh's hand, and was grateful when he put an arm around her and let her lean into his shoulder.

"Are you sure you're okay?" Josh asked.

She nodded.

For a moment he looked away, then his eyes came back to her. "We could go to my room if you want to get away from all this. My roommate hasn't gotten here yet."

Winnie felt a strong wave of dizziness. Everything in her vision spun and mushed together.

Josh led her away from the dancers and into the hallway that led to their rooms. A few doors were open, revealing more music and laughter and groups of people collected for smaller, more intimate parties.

Josh took off his tennis shoe and dumped out his room key. When he opened the door, Winnie saw a room exactly like hers, except that half the room was empty. Josh's half had an Navajo blanket over his bed, a cassette player, a computer and boxes and boxes of floppy disks, a basketball, and some strange-looking pieces of electronic equipment with wires and circuit boards exposed. Josh stuck in a tape of ragtime piano, but instead of coming back over to her, he stood by his desk, watching her.

"How do you feel?"

"Great. Thirsty." Her throat was parched. She tried to swallow.

Josh went to the door. "Do you want me to run down to the basement and get a couple of sodas from the machine?" He smiled.

Winnie shook her head. "No, thanks. I'll be okay."

For a moment Josh stayed in the doorway. Finally he closed the door.

The noise from the party sounded very far away, and in the stillness Winnie felt even more woozy and hot. She was suddenly conscious that both she and Josh were dressed mainly in bedsheets. Her knees buckled and she stumbled toward Josh's bed.

He still stood, looking at her. "You sure you feel okay?"

"I feel great." She patted the blanket, which was thick and soft. "Sit down."

He came over slowly and sat on the bed next to

her. For a moment they sat side by side, listening to the other breathe. Then Winnie laid her head against Josh's smooth, warm shoulder.

Josh began to kiss the top of her head—little, light kisses that made her eyes close and her head loll until she turned and met his mouth. As Winnie lay back on his bed, the room began to spin. She had a brief flash back to her summer, a brief warning and moment of regret, but the rum blocked it out. Instead there were the muffled party sounds, the soft blanket, and the spicy smell of Josh's aftershave.

In a second, Winnie realized that the music had completely faded away. Instead she felt a swirling sensation along with dizzying heat and a dark fluidity in her brain. But even more powerful was the feel of Josh's chest as he pulled her closer and wrapped her tightly in his arms.

Eleven

It was quiet when Faith got back to Coleridge Hall. No one was singing or tap dancing. There were no heated discussions in the lounge about great books and the meaning of art.

Lying on her bed in the total silence, Faith stared out the window at the dark, her chin in her hands. She felt lost and frightened. When Lauren stuck her key in the door, it sounded like the opening of an ancient iron-doored prison cell.

Lauren walked in. "You're still up," she said in an expressionless voice.

"It's not late."

"Oh, I guess it isn't."

It was barely eleven. The toga party was still in full swing, which was why Coleridge was so quiet and calm. Faith had come back early, despite the hurt on Brooks's face. She had been unable to stick it out, unable to pretend that she was having a terrific time.

Lauren put her jacket on the back of her desk chair and it slid to the floor, making a loud noise in the quiet room. "Sorry."

"For what?"

"For disturbing you. You look like you want to be alone."

"It's your room, too, Lauren."

"I know." Lauren found her contact lens solution and a zippered cosmetic bag. She gathered her nightgown and towel and, with the tiniest glance back at Faith, padded out again.

Faith sensed that Lauren was upset, and she had the urge to follow her roommate down the hall. But her slender body felt too heavy to pick up off the bed. And she couldn't stop thinking.

"I have to remember," she told herself aloud.

Faith had been straining to recall how she and Brooks had gotten together. She wanted to remember the exact moment when that spark had flickered to life. Most couples could recount every detail of their first blind date or pinpoint the time they had looked at each other over a chemistry beaker and bingo! They could say what had drawn them together, what kept them on track, and where they were going in the future.

But with Brooks and her it had never happened that way. They had no anniversary, no sole common interest, no special song. They'd been in the same classes all through middle school. After that Brooks and Faith began walking home together, even though Brooks's father and stepmom had a ranch almost a mile the other way. Then somewhere around ninth grade they'd started dancing together at school dances and sitting together at assemblies. They did things on weekends and pretty soon it was all set. They were a couple.

The door opened again and Lauren came back, carrying her contact lens case and bringing with her the smell of shampoo and baby powder. The shower had taken the poofiness from her hair. She was wearing wire-rimmed glasses, and from what Faith could tell her eyes really were an amazing violet color.

"Hi, again," Lauren said, a little self-consciously. She hung up her clothes and crawled onto her bed in her nightgown.

A pause followed. Faith knew she couldn't mention her confusion about Brooks. Even though the college computer had put her and Lauren in the same room, they were still strangers.

"How was the toga party?" Lauren took her journal notebook from the bin above her bed.

Faith didn't answer. "How was rush?"

"If it weren't for my mom, Tri Beta wouldn't want me."

"That's not true."

"Yes, it is."

The wind gusted, pushing the branches of the oak tree against the window. Faith and Lauren listened to the soft, swooshing sound.

"Why do you have to rush at all?" Faith suggested, pushing thoughts of Brooks further back into her mind. "Why don't you just stay in the dorms after this year?"

Lauren smiled sadly. "Good question. Well, I see the way you and Winnie and KC are together, and I think that's the kind of sisterhood I want to be in."

Faith shook her head.

"Maybe it'll get better. Everything feels like it's changing so fast." Lauren sighed.

"It does, doesn't it?" Faith looked up. Freya must have just gotten home, because a soprano's voice drifted in from next door.

Lauren looked over, too. "I keep thinking about something my prep-school writing teacher told us."

"What was that?"

"He said that change meant danger and opportunity. He said it was up to us to decide which way we were going to go."

"Danger *and* opportunity?"

"I don't know." Lauren shook her head and closed her journal. "Maybe he was wrong." Both girls were quiet while footsteps clomped down the hall and into one of the rooms.

Faith sat a while longer, thinking about what Lauren's teacher had said. *Danger and opportunity.* She looked at her old stuffed bear on the window sill, her new book bag hanging over the back of her chair. She didn't think of change as dangerous. Sad, maybe. Actually, she felt nostalgia for the safe, old times of high school. The prom. Hiking with Brooks in Jacksonville Park. The times she, KC, and Winnie had cut school and gone to Lassen Lake.

"You want some popcorn?" Lauren asked.

"Why not?"

They scrambled out of bed and broke into Lauren's stash of microwave popcorn. Soon pop pops were firing off like machine-gun fire and the smell of overcooked butter filled the room. Just as the bell went off to tell them that the popcorn was ready, there was a knock at the door.

"Wouldn't you know," Faith managed to joke. "People always stop by when it's dinner time."

Lauren knelt down in front of the microwave and pulled out the balloon of popcorn. With tentative fingers she broke the cellophane and tasted the corn.

"Come in," Faith called.

The door didn't open. Instead, the knock continued, getting more elaborate and musical, like someone playing a drum.

"Who is it?" Lauren asked.

A moment later there was music outside the door. The knocking started again, in time to the music.

"It's got to be one of our floormates," said Faith. "Maybe it's Freya or Kimberly."

"Or Winnie," Faith and Lauren decided at the same time. Faith went to the door and opened it. But it wasn't Winnie.

"Good evening."

It wasn't anyone that Faith recognized from Coleridge or Forest or even the old dorm where KC lived. Standing there was a good-looking guy with a dark mustache. At least twenty, he was wearing a crested navy sport coat and a paisley tie. On his left hand he wore a big, chunky ring, and he held a tape player. Faith knew that she had met him before, but she couldn't remember when or where.

"Mark Geisslinger," he reminded her, bowing

like someone from another century. He swaggered into the doorway and winked.

She remembered that it was Christopher Hammond's roommate from the fraternity. But what was Christopher's roommate doing at her door at that hour of night?

Faith glanced back at Lauren, who'd hurried back into bed and was pulling the covers over herself as if she wanted to disappear. Usually Faith wouldn't give her looks a second thought, but something about Mark's gaze made her feel almost as self-conscious as Lauren. She pushed back a few stray hairs.

When the song finished Mark turned off the tape player and pulled a playing card out of his jacket pocket. He stepped further into their room and held up the card, which was the king of hearts.

"This is a formal request," Mark began, his eyes shifting from Faith to Lauren, "for your presence tomorrow night at the Omega Delta Tau house party. Make sure to bring this card and arrive by eight o'clock. When you get to the party, your date will have a card that matches this one. And that's how you'll know that you are his dream date."

Faith had heard about the dream date dance from KC. She remembered that guys asked girls for their roommates. She also knew how secretive the choosing was—the way so much of what she considered to be sorority and fraternity nonsense was surrounded by tradition and secrecy.

She could hardly believe it. Was it possible that Christopher was arranging to go out with her through his roommate? She was almost woozy. She hadn't realized—until that startling moment—she had been thinking and daydreaming about Christopher.

Mark placed the card on the nearest desk. "So, Lauren Turnbell-Smythe, Omega Delta Tau and your dream date request your lovely presence tomorrow night. We hope you can fit it into your rush schedule. Please do not disappoint us." He winked again. "Good night."

Faith almost cried out. Her body felt as if it were collapsing inside as Mark walked away. Was she insane? How had Christopher even entered her head? The Greek traditions were never extended to mere dorm dwellers like her. Only a potential sorority sister would be eligible for the dream date dance. And what had made her have those sudden, overpowering thoughts about Christopher? When she finally felt that she could face Lauren again, she turned around.

Lauren was standing over her desk, glasses back on, staring down at the King of Hearts as though it were likely to blow up. For a long time neither of them said a word.

"Why does this make me feel so scared?" Lauren finally asked.

Faith could still barely catch her breath. She was scared, too. Absolutely terrified. "I don't know. Why?"

"My dream date. He's probably the only complete loser in ODT."

"Why do you think that?"

Lauren picked up the card, her eyes full of doubt.

Faith tried to hide her disappointment. "I think it's wonderful."

Lauren stared at the playing card. "The sorority sister I had an interview with said I had to do something to show them I was Tri Beta material. Maybe this is it," she said, gaining confidence. Suddenly, she collapsed in her desk chair. "Faith," she breathed. "What if it's Christopher Hammond?"

Faith was unable to speak.

Lauren let her head fall on her folded arms and moaned. "I think I'll call my mother and spend tomorrow night with her." Then she lifted her head, and a smile spread over her face. She reached for a handful of popcorn and chucked it into the air. "Or maybe I won't. Maybe my old writing teacher was right. Talk about danger and opportunity."

Faith nodded, trying to regain her voice. But as Lauren grew more and more excited, finally flicking popcorn in the air, Faith just stood there, paralyzed.

What was going on? How could she have gotten so crazy over the possibility of a date with Christopher when she was supposed to be in love with Brooks? Maybe college *was* a time for change, for going after something new, starting over. But this was scary. This was a major overhaul. A complete destruction of everything from the past.

Faith made her way to the window, away from the kernels of popped corn that had fallen about the room. She stared out into the dark. *Danger and opportunity.* It was clear which category Christopher Hammond fell into. Danger. Real danger. Trying to hook her heart back up to Brooks, Faith grabbed her old stuffed bear and hugged it to her chest.

Twelve

Even with her eyes closed, Winnie was aware of thin, grainy early-morning light falling across her face. Her head felt as if someone had gone bowling between her ears. Her mouth tasted awful. When she finally sat up, she immediately wished she hadn't.

"Ohh . . ." she moaned.

Gray light was filtering through the dorm room window. It made Winnie blink. Then she felt the first wave of nausea. She wondered if she was sick and tried to recall what they had told her about using the health center. Then she remembered. *The rum. The toga dance. The—*

She lifted her head. She was in her room. She

recognized the cottage cheese ceiling, the orange carpet and clean beige walls.

Except . . .

If it was her room, why was there a computer on her desk? Where were her incense sticks and Melissa's books and the wildflowers she had picked the afternoon before?

Winnie sat up with a jolt as more memories flooded back. "Uh-oh," she mumbled. Then she heard a sigh. She turned her head and saw the other single bed that had been moved next to hers. Still asleep in that bed, Josh rolled over, reaching for her as he moved. There were rumpled sheets and blankets everywhere.

Winnie tore at the sheets twisted around her legs until finally she could move. It was only then that she began to move more slowly, as she watched Josh stir and grumble and almost wake up. She began to realize how little she really knew about him, and how she didn't have the faintest idea what to do next.

So she sat very still and thought about what had happened that summer. She thought about Travis Bennett in Paris. Travis had been Winnie's very first lover. Even though Winnie had always acted like she'd really been around, and even though her mother had taken her to get birth control pills on her sixteenth birthday, Winnie had waited until she was on her own. Her mother pushed so hard for her to be adventurous and independent that it had almost the opposite effect: when Winnie was home, she had to fight the urge to stay alone in her room, read horror novels, and watch TV.

Winnie had met Travis her first week abroad, in—of all places!—the Paris Burger King. She'd felt so lonely and Travis had been funny and good-looking, with long hair and a scraggly beard that he was just starting to grow. He was staying in a little hotel, and Winnie had decided that it was time. So she went to his room. Travis had been gentle, and made jokes to ease her nerves. Winnie had been surprised at the feelings he provoked in her. And since she was scared and had doubts about how much he really cared in return, she threw herself into the romance, barely leaving his room for two and a half days. When she finally did leave, so did he. Travis left for Spain. And then he left for Italy. And then for who knows where because after a few phone calls and a couple of weeks, Winnie never heard from him again. She spent the rest of her summer abroad staying inside, alone, watching French TV.

"Josh," Winnie whispered weakly, hoping that he wouldn't answer her. "Josh."

She watched him sleep. He had the blanket tucked up under his chin, like a little kid. His mouth was open slightly. For a split second he smiled and murmured something in his sleep. Then he turned over. His hair fell over his forehead, and his bare arm hung down over the side of the bed, almost touching the floor.

Winnie started to get a strange feeling deep in her chest. For an awful second she thought she was going to be sick, horribly sick right in the middle of Josh's bed. Instead, she started to cry. Tears ran down her face, although she didn't make a sound. She was afraid to wake Josh up, and yet she wanted to keep sitting there. She wanted him to smile again, to somehow stay sound asleep yet tell her everything she desperately needed to know.

What exactly had happened? What had she said? What did it mean? How did he really feel about her?

What was going to happen next?

Winnie thought back to the reassuring moments—the moments she remembered clearly. Like when she had met Josh on the lawn during the Frisbee game, and when she had kissed him in the lobby the night before. Those moments came back to her with overpowering force. She remembered how she'd thrown herself at him and how he'd tried to slow her down. The way it had felt when he'd put his hand to her cheek . . . Winnie would never forget that.

She had really messed things up, she thought. She had pretended to be wild and flip, when in reality she felt as serious about him as she really felt about college—and about herself.

Winnie wrapped her own sheet more tightly around her and inched to the end of the bed, so that she could get up without disturbing him. Then she tiptoed to the door, praying that Josh would not wake up. As quietly as possible, she opened the door. There was no Z card on the outside of it, but that didn't necessarily mean anything. Z cards were messages to roommates and Josh knew his roommate wasn't arriving until just before classes began.

Hugging her sheet to her clammy skin, she peeked out into the hall. As far as she could tell, the coast was clear. She started down toward her room. She passed the bathrooms, heard the rumble of the shower, and kept on going. She found her room key on the ribbon around her neck and stuck it in the lock.

"Have a good night?"

It was a guy dressed only in track shorts, leaving the men's lavatory and drying his hair with a towel. His tone was suggestive.

She looked him right in the eye and managed to smile. "Did I ever."

He laughed, and Winnie thought she might start to cry again. Instead, she let herself into her room.

When she heard the key rattle, Melissa McDormand muttered to herself, "How much more of this am I supposed to take?"

Out of the corner of her eye, she watched her roommate stagger into the room, drop her wrinkled toga sheet on the floor, and put on her nightclothes. Melissa pulled the blanket over her head, which reminded her again that she had no top sheet. She muttered under her breath. Pretending to be asleep, she inched her wrist up to her face and checked the face of her watch. It was 5:12 A.M.

Winnie tripped on something. "Come on," she swore. She turned on her lamp. "There," she whispered loudly. She knocked over something on her dresser, then lit her incense.

Melissa wanted to scream.

The day she arrived, Melissa had been so excited to meet her college roommate that she went out and bought jelly beans, then arranged them on Winnie's bed. She still wasn't sure why she'd picked jelly beans, except that she'd wanted to do something nice for her new roommate, and jelly beans were on sale right in front of her. But had Winnie even thanked her for the gesture? Had she even bothered to wake up early enough to say hello?

There was more noise. Winnie was putting a bottle of makeup remover back down on the dresser. She didn't just place it, she slammed it down, and the cap fell to the floor. Winnie opened a drawer, then slammed it shut. She took off her earrings. *Plunk. Clink. Dink.* In the quiet of the morning it sounded like rocks being dropped into a metal bowl. Melissa sighed loudly and turned over, hoping that Winnie would get the message.

Winnie flopped onto her creaky bed, then opened a book and noisily flipped through the pages.

Rage and frustration were building inside Melissa. All she wanted was to sleep so she could be at track workout before seven. She was on an athletic scholarship, so she literally couldn't afford to do anything but her best. She wondered what kind of girl would take college so lightly that she'd be out almost all night during her very first week.

Winnie sighed and peered out the window. She muttered something that sounded like a blur between "Should I?" and "What now?"

"I can't take this," Melissa murmured after pulling the blanket up even higher over her head. It was bad enough to be in a party dorm. The last thing she needed was a party roommate. "It's not fair."

Melissa threw back her blanket and sat up. She stared at Winnie, who she realized was rather petite. Winnie's hair was uncombed. Her make up was smudged and she looked dreadfully tired.

Winnie put a hand to her face as if she'd just seen a ghost. She gasped. "Oh. Hello."

For a few moments they stared at each other. Melissa sat up and swung her feet onto the floor.

"Did I wake you?" Winnie asked in a weak voice.

It was such an understatement that Melissa nearly laughed out loud. It was five in the morning and she was beginning to feel like she was in the middle of a nightmare—no sleep, no top sheet, and the ever-growing mess that she had to wade through every morning and night. She got out of bed and started picking up Winnie's clothes.

"What are you doing?"

"I can't take it anymore," Melissa barked. "I can barely make it to the bathroom without breaking my leg." Melissa picked up college brochures, pairs of tights, bras, slippers, and horror novels, and put them in a pile at the foot of Winnie's bed.

"I'm sorry," Winnie said.

"Sorry doesn't help."

Winnie put her hands to her head. "I don't know why you're so upset."

"Why shouldn't I be upset?" Melissa said accusingly. "This room is a mess. You come in at all hours. And what in the world made you think you could take my sheet? You are totally inconsiderate!"

"I said I was sorry."

"Great."

Winnie was starting to look even paler. "Look, I really am sorry about the mess and the sheet and everything. I didn't realize that you were so upset about it."

"Well, you should have."

Winnie stared at Melissa for a long time. Then she admitted, "I can't talk about it right now. I don't feel very well." She went back over to her bed and folded down onto it. She mumbled into her hands, "I have a terrible hangover."

Melissa felt every muscle in her body grow tense. "That's just swell."

Tears welled up in Winnie's eyes.

Melissa swept her towel off the hook on the door and marched out. The last thing she heard before heading to the shower was Winnie turning into her pillow and beginning to cry.

Thirteen

The university Mill Pond was beautiful. Long willow branches touched the water like gentle fingers. Ducks paraded behind swans, which cruised back and forth over the green water with the unmistakable air of proprietorship.

Faith stood in line at the boathouse Friday morning with Lauren and KC, waiting to be issued paddles and a canoe. The freshmen were lined up all the way past the boathouse and out to the Volcanology Building. But Faith had gotten a place early, so they wouldn't have much of a wait.

"Faith, can we get a big canoe?" Lauren asked.

"Why?" KC asked. "There are only three of us. We can fit into a little one."

"We need a big one." Faith peered out across the pond. Robins flew under the canopy of surrounding trees. "We're waiting for Winnie."

"Well," KC cracked, "be prepared to wait until midterms. Winnie was supposed to meet me at breakfast, but she never showed up. And I was even ready to apologize for being so critical of her! It's useless to wait."

"KC, she's just late. You know Winnie."

"Do I ever. Teen genius who acts like a total dummy." KC's eyes scanned the dock.

When they got to the front of the line, Faith made sure they were issued four paddles and a big canoe. Without help, she pulled the canoe to the dock so they could get in.

KC and Lauren followed, watching while Faith set up the boat.

KC extended her hand toward the canoe, grinning at Lauren. "After you, future Tri Beta."

"No, af-tah you," Lauren responded in a phony British accent.

Laughing, they pretended to push each other toward the green water, while Faith held onto the boat and secured the paddles. Both Lauren and KC were in great moods.

"Tonight is the dream date dance at ODT," KC

reminded Lauren. They stepped into the canoe, taking great care not to get a drop of water on their clothes. "No more interviews until tomorrow night, which is the big interview before the entire house. I know we're going to get in. I can just feel it."

"I still can't believe Mark handed me that playing card," Lauren said. Her lovely pale skin had flushed pink across her cheeks.

"Believe it," KC said. She grabbed the side of the canoe and very carefully made her way to the little back seat. "Faith, are you sure you can handle the paddling? We'd help, except we have to be ready in case any sisters want to check up on us."

"I know." Faith wished that KC would forget about the stupid Tri Betas. And she was annoyed by the way she put down Winnie. But she couldn't dwell on either because she had more important things to worry about.

All night Faith had been thinking about Brooks. She couldn't remember when or how they had gotten together. Theirs had never been a passionate romance, but Faith reminded herself Brooks was a great person. He cared about her. They had a lot of history together and she was a fool to even think about anything that might bust them apart.

Faith scoured the crowd of freshmen boaters hoping to see Brooks's handsome face again, so that all her doubts would disappear. She saw lots of freshmen wandering weak legged and bleary eyed from last night's party. She heard water lap the sides of the canoe. Speckled light fell through the tree branches. A butterfly was making graceful curves over the water, when Faith heard a familiar scream.

"YOU GUYS!"

There was no mistaking the voice. Winnie sounded elated. No, more than elated; she sounded manic, so overly excited that she could hardly stand it. She was running, wearing silky shorts and a halter top. Heads turned as her exposed, terrific body jumped and raced along the dock, dodging other freshmen, putting her hands on the waists of guys to move them aside. Soon she stood over Faith's canoe. "What a morning."

"You made it," stated KC.

"Did you ever doubt it?"

Winnie stuck her jogging shoe into the water and kicked, raising a crescent of wet, gooey green. Nearby two ducks dunked their heads, went bottoms up and paddled their feet. KC shrank back, rocking the canoe.

Then Winnie kalumphed into the boat, making it sway even more.

"Winnie, be careful!" KC protested.

"It's just water. You won't melt." Winnie

grabbed an oar, then leaned almost flat to her back and kissed KC on the cheek. "Sorry." Only then did Faith notice the heavy makeup under Winnie's eyes. She wondered if Winnie were terribly tired, or even a little sick, but Winnie's sky-high mood continued. "I'm so completely, incredibly happy this morning that even you, KC—my ex–best friend who suddenly thinks everything I do is wrong—even you cannot bring me down."

Faith and Lauren perked up, ignoring the tension between Winnie and KC and eager to know why Winnie was so ecstatic. Even KC smiled guiltily. Winnie made them wait while she and Faith pushed off with their paddles and the boat began to glide out into the pond. The air smelled like grass and warm sunshine.

"*Yippee!*" Winnie yelled to the sky.

A duck quacked in reply. They all laughed.

"So?" Faith and Lauren asked at the same time, when they'd made their way out into Mill Pond proper.

"What happened, Win?" prompted KC. "Are you going to tell us? Why are you so excited?"

Winnie looked coy. Then she laughed, a loud laugh that sounded a little forced. "Guess."

"You won the lottery," said KC.

"You finally met mysterious Melissa and she's

really your long-lost friend from first grade," said Faith.

At the mention of Melissa's name, some of the excitement left Winnie's face, and for a moment she looked upset. "Um, no," she said.

"Well, what?"

Winnie looked around the pond and a grin returned to her face. Other canoes were slicing through the water, trying to stay out of one another's paths. More and more boats were taking off from the dock, weaving their way around the pond.

They paddled a few more strokes and Winnie finally squealed, "Last night. Me and Josh." That was all she said before throwing her head back and shrieking at the sun.

"You and Josh what?"

"That guy in your dorm? Did he ask you out?"

"What?"

Winnie took her paddle out of the water and rested it across the gunwales. In a low, clear voice she said, "I spent the night with him. The whole night."

When she was greeted by stunned silence, she added, "And it was great."

KC stared.

Lauren gasped.

Faith worried.

The canoe stalled aimlessly as they all hoisted their paddles out of the water.

"Win, you barely know him," KC ventured.

Lauren looked back at the shore, as if the conversation were too intimate for her to take part.

Winnie shrugged at KC's comment, then put on a grin and flicked water at her. "It's one way to get to know someone, KC. It changes a relationship. Real fast."

Faith was staring at Winnie, too. "Does it?"

It was so quiet they could hear the water lap at the sides of the boat.

"Does it make everything different?" Faith asked again.

"Does it, Win?" KC asked in a softer voice.

Winnie's face grew serious. "It can. It can make you feel really close to someone. And, um, it can make you feel really far away."

"Which was it?" KC wanted to know.

Winnie looked right at her. She tossed off her seriousness and grinned again. "Guess!"

"Winnie!"

Winnie laughed and grabbed her paddle. "Josh is wonderful. He's even smart and nice and everything."

Then Faith and KC began paddling, too. The *dip*, *dip*, *dip* of the paddles could be heard as the canoe moved ahead.

Faith was still reeling from Winnie's pronouncement. She worried that Winnie had gone way too far again and was only going to get hurt. And yet another part of her had to wonder if Winnie didn't have the right idea. Maybe it was her own fault that her relationship with Brooks had stalled. Faith had never slept with Brooks, except for camping out once when they'd zipped their sleeping bags together and fooled around. But it hadn't gone that far. They hadn't made love. Maybe they needed to get closer. Maybe they needed to make that kind of change.

Still, Faith wasn't sure. She didn't feel prepared. Sure, Winnie's mother had given them all a lecture about birth control and being safe, and had made them all go to Thrifty's and buy condoms. But then there were all the movies, that made it look so spontaneous and romantic. Kissing on the bed. Fade out. Cut. Morning after with the couple looking so happy. So changed.

They coasted under some trees with low branches. Winnie picked leaves as they went by and began decorating Lauren's hair. Both girls laughed. Meanwhile, other canoes were circling in the center of the pond, sending the swans and ducks off in all directions.

Just then some girls started slapping their paddles into the water, initiating a splash fight with two boys in an old red canoe. More canoes joined, and soon a solo boater gave a holler and toppled into the water.

"Here I come!" someone yelled.

"No one's safe," called someone else.

"Bombs away!"

Other boats headed for the action, as if water fights were really the secret agenda of the outing. Faith recognized her dormmates Kimberly, Beth, and Dante in a little blue canoe. They tried to weave their way through the middle of the fray, but bumped into a large boat and flipped, shrieking with joy. They kicked and swam over to the big canoe, trying to upset it.

In the back of the boat, KC was getting frantic. "Let's go back!" she ordered. "Right now. Don't get near another boat."

Faith and Winnie tried to obey, but they were not very skillful at turning the canoe around. Furthermore, the water fight was expanding. A jock from Forest stood up in his boat, yodeling like Tarzan as his canoe rocked and finally flipped. The splashing and kicking was getting so wild that no canoe seemed out of bounds.

That was when Winnie yelled out, *"Josh!"*

She pointed at a dark head, bobbing up and down in the water, then looked back at the girls.

"That's him," she said, looking a little paler. "That's Josh. I knew it was him."

"I don't think he sees you," Lauren said, leaning to look and almost tipping the canoe.

"Careful," KC warned.

"Oops." Lauren giggled.

Then a two-man canoe from Brooks's dorm came perilously close and slapped a spray of water in their direction. Faith stopped paddling and crouched down in the boat, protecting herself and laughing at the same time. She tried to spot Brooks.

"Josh!" Winnie screamed again.

She was answered by a whap of water.

"Stop," KC pleaded. "Please don't."

One side of Lauren's jumpsuit was soaked but, unlike KC, she wasn't upset. She was laughing, sticking her hand in the mucky water, and threatening to fight back.

"Josh!" Winnie yelled one more time.

Faith heard a trace of desperation in Winnie's voice. She wasn't laughing anymore, either. She felt a little desperate herself, trying to locate Brooks through the shower of pond water and worrying about KC.

"Winnie, can't you wait until we get back to the dock?" KC demanded. "Let's go back *now*."

"We'll never make it back dry, KC. I'm sorry, but it's not my fault. Face it. You're all wet.

There's nothing I can do." A four-man Forest canoe was heading right for them. Winnie threw down her paddle and stood up in the canoe.

"We're toast," Winnie yelled. *"Ahhhh!"*

"Hold on, Winnie—" Faith started to say.

But Winnie didn't seem to hear her. The Forest canoe paddled closer and closer, sending bigger and bigger waves toward them. In a flash, Winnie plunged into the water. She bobbed up and looked around, then her head went under again and she began a relentless crawl stroke.

Winnie's dive had been made with sufficient force to push Faith's side of the canoe completely under water. Faith, Lauren, and KC made the mistake of trying to regain their balance simultaneously. Their actions worked against one another and the next thing Faith knew, they were all in the water.

"Winnie!" KC screamed.

Winnie didn't hear KC yell, because her ears were under water. But it wouldn't have mattered. No matter whose fault it was, KC would have blamed her.

Winnie kept swimming. She'd just seen Josh pull himself, dripping wet, back into a small aluminum canoe. She needed to talk to him, or just to look into his eyes. She still wasn't sure if last night was the best or the worst evening of her life.

She swam up to Josh's canoe and clung to the side.

"Hey!" said Josh, recognizing her. He tossed back his wet hair, flinging beads of pond water. He looked well rested and healthy, with a little sunburn on his nose and the tops of his shoulders. "Winnie!" he said.

"Hi."

"The disappearing Winnie." He looked at her and must have noticed the circles under her eyes and the pallor of her cheeks. "How are you feeling?"

"Great," she said instantly. She smoothed back her wet hair and hung on to the side of his canoe.

Josh didn't seem to believe her. "You sure you're all right? You were pretty drunk last night."

Instead of responding, she took a quick dip under the water. When she surfaced again, he helped her climb into the boat. He wanted to find out how she really felt, but she started talking instead.

"Great day, huh?" she said quickly. "My friend KC is probably going to kill me because I tipped our boat, but we would have gotten tipped anyway, and how can you go canoeing and not get soaked? Anyway, I always like being in the middle of the action. It's the only place to be. So I took the plunge, so to speak."

Josh smiled. He liked Winnie's spunk and humor. He was curious about her, even attracted to her—very attracted. But he wasn't sure how to relate to someone bent on reciting a monologue he couldn't quite follow. He sat back in the sun and watched her.

"Anyway," she chattered on, "I saw you and had to say hello. After last night. Which was pretty great."

"Huh?"

"I mean, weird. Pretty weird."

"Parts of it were great. Parts were weird," Josh said, trying to figure out what she meant.

"Yeah, well," she went on, filling in the quiet spaces, "it doesn't matter. That's what college is like, huh? Lots of great, weird nights."

"I guess."

"I *know*." Winnie laughed. "Because I had plenty of weird and wonderful nights in France this summer, too. I don't know if I can remember them all. The guys and the nights."

Josh looked off. At first he had thought he might really fall for Winnie, in spite of the fact that he didn't want to get involved with someone right away, and that he didn't care much for girls who drank. "Lots of guys?" he asked.

Winnie paused. Then she smiled and winked. "And lots of nights."

Something inside Josh tensed up. He'd suspected last night that Winnie came on too easily, that she might be a girl who used guys for entertainment, that she didn't really care. But her face had said something else. So had the way she kissed, and the confused sweetness he saw in her eyes. Now he wondered if his initial suspicions had been right.

"Well, I guess your great nights in France were a little more exciting than last night," he said. "At least I hope they were."

"What?"

Josh looked closely and saw something else in Winnie's face. Bewilderment, embarrassment—maybe a combination of the two. "I mean, when you drink a lot, it makes things pretty weird. That's all."

The water fight had moved farther across the pond. They both looked off in the direction of the shouts.

"Was it awful?" Winnie suddenly asked in a barely audible voice.

"Was what awful?"

Winnie went even paler.

When she didn't answer, it finally hit him. She'd drunk so much that she'd blacked out. She didn't remember the previous night at all. "Winnie, it wasn't awful. You just kissed me and then you passed out. I covered you with my blanket and watched you sleep for a while."

Winnie's mouth fell open, and then she put her hand over her eyes. "Oh, my God."

"It was okay," he reassured her. "You didn't throw up or anything. I think you snored once or twice, though."

Josh had hoped to make her laugh, but she wouldn't even look at him. He began to paddle again. They glided under the bridge, silently watching some little kids fishing from the top of it.

Winnie kept her back to him. Finally she turned around and reached for a paddle. Josh hoped she'd want to know more about what had happened—and what hadn't happened. but instead she forced a laugh. "Do you want me to help? Hey, maybe I should start training for one of those triathlon things where they run, swim and bike. Oops, I guess boating isn't part of that. Oh, well. I guess there's a lot of things I don't remember."

Josh was heading back toward the dock. With each awkward moment, the shore got closer and closer.

He wasn't sure what to do next. He wished he could say, *Winnie, this is too weird. Let's start all over again.* But instead he told her, "Winnie, I'm really glad that you're doing okay, but I have an orientation meeting at the computer center. I have to go. If you want, you can keep the canoe and paddle around some more."

He saw something like hurt race across Winnie's face, but her smile remained pasted on. He wasn't sure if she was disappointed that he was leaving, or relieved.

Josh dipped his paddle in once more and they slid toward the bank. Once there he climbed out slowly and pulled the boat to the dock.

"I guess I'll stick around here and find my friends," she said. "If they still are my friends," she added, a little sadly.

Josh helped Winnie out. He held her a little longer than necessary and looked into her eyes. Something inside him was still stirred by her, but he felt that they needed to start over. He tousled her wet hair and said, "Why don't you go back to Forest and get some rest?"

"Sure."

"We'll see each other later."

"Right."

"I'm glad you're feeling okay."

"Yeah."

He walked away with his T-shirt thrown over his bare back.

Fourteen

Back in the center of Mill Pond, Faith was still fighting it out—kicking, ambushing, dumping, tipping, and splashing. She'd seen KC swim to the nearby shore and angrily climb out. Lauren had gotten in a few good splashes, then hitched a ride back with some Coleridge people.

The water was murky and cold, but Faith needed to do *something*. Tipping canoes was crazy, but Faith had the feeling that if she didn't do something crazy pretty soon, she might come apart at the seams.

She was dogpaddling, sneaking up behind the

Rapids Hall boat, when it all came together for her. Brooks. Winnie. Change. Christopher.

"Faith, is that you?"

Faith knew instantly that it was Brooks. He was in a two-man boat with Barney, who had his shirt off and was oiled with so much suntan lotion that Faith feared for the health of the fish if he got thrown in. Brooks and Barney were paddling toward another canoe.

In a matter of seconds Faith was head-first into the pond and swimming like an otter. She popped out of the water at the front of Brooks's canoe. She reached as far out of the water as she could, then pushed with all her weight on the front of the canoe.

Brooks toppled off his seat. His mouth fell open. "Faith!"

"It's me," she squealed, then swam under, coming up again at the side, where she started rocking the boat as fiercely as she could. Brooks held on and watched her, confused, until Barney dove in after her. A moment later, Brooks followed.

Barney caught Faith first. His arms were so thick it was like being wrestled by a giant octopus. Faith laughed and stuck her feet in his muscular stomach, pushing her way loose. Brooks took over. He'd whipped off his shirt before diving, and as he grabbed Faith she could feel his strong, slippery chest against her back. His curly hair dripped water as he held onto her and teased, "You asked for it, Faith!"

"Oh, yeah?" Faith put her hands on Brooks's shoulders and pushed him under. He came back up and hugged her waist, twisting her in the water. He finally tossed her a few feet away, then grabbed her ankle.

Faith tried to free her leg, laughing and coughing and trying to talk at the same time. But underneath her playfulness, part of her was thinking seriously.

She knew it was time to go for broke. Winnie had done it, and now it was time for her and Brooks, too. That's was what was missing. That was the difference between high school and college. Between old and new. Between holding back and diving in.

She and Brooks were going to sleep together. Really sleep together.

That night.

She threw herself back across the water and swung her arms around Brooks's naked torso. He tossed his head back and laughed. Finally they both caught their breath and looked into each other's wet, dripping faces.

"I have to talk to you tonight," she insisted between gulps and coughs.

"Okay."

"I mean, I have to see you tonight."

He suddenly pushed her under again, then swam after her and grabbed the hem of her T-shirt. Cold water flooded against her stomach. Then Brooks pulled her close to him and Faith felt her bare skin against his.

"Let's get together for dinner. Not at the dining commons," she said.

"What's the matter?" Brooks chortled. "Already had your fill of Salisbury steak?"

"Yum," they said at the same time.

They both gave up their struggle and drifted back to the side of the canoe. They hung on and caught their breath.

"I'm serious. I have an evening planned." Faith blushed. "I mean, I'm going to plan an evening."

Brooks smiled. "That's a good idea. Things have been feeling kind of weird the last few days."

"I know."

"So I'll come by for you at seven?"

Faith dipped her head back in the water so that her hair was slicked back like a helmet. "No," she surprised herself by saying. "I'll come by for you."

"And then?"

Faith laughed. "And then we'll see what happens."

Brooks stared at her, a little perplexed, but Faith didn't care. She leaned toward Brooks and kissed him on the mouth—a wet, deep, slippery kiss. Then she smiled and ran her hand slowly down the side of his strong face.

The other water fighters stopped splashing to gawk, but Brooks didn't say anything right away. He looked a little stunned. "I'll see you tonight," he finally said.

"You will," Faith said, breaking away from the canoe and letting go of him. She dogpaddled a little bit, waved, and then dove under the water. Smiling to herself, she swam as fast as she could all the way back to the dock.

In the women's bathroom next to the boathouse, twenty freshmen girls were drying off and changing. Courtney Conner was there, too, impeccably dressed and waiting for KC.

"I didn't come over here trying to catch you," Courtney said. "I know how these orientation week things can be."

KC was shivering. Her dress was stuck to every part of her body, and her hair looked like seaweed. After spotting Courtney strolling around the dock, KC had thought she would be safe in the bathroom. But Courtney had found her anyway. KC was beginning to see her brilliant future go swirling down the drain. Maybe her parents' restaurant was all she was cut out for. Maybe she was destined to spend her life serving platters of eggplant and whole-wheat rolls.

Courtney inched aside to make room for two giggling freshmen who were wringing out their socks. "I only came here to ask if you could go over to ODT and help with decorations for the dance tonight. I know you're supposed to be ready for inspection all the time, but I think that custom is a little silly. Still, it puts me in a difficult position."

"I know," KC said. She caught another glimpse of herself in the mirror and barely recognized the dripping girl she saw there. "It's my friends. I only went canoeing because I wanted to talk to one of my friends. I won't do it again."

"That's another thing I wanted to talk to you about," Courtney interrupted. She pulled KC into a corner near the stalls, away from the sinks and the giggly banter. "Your friend."

How could KC explain that even though Winnie was flaky and thoughtless, she had stuck by KC all through high school? KC had been trying to put some distance between Winnie and herself, but it wasn't that simple.

"I didn't want to see *her* like this, either," Courtney continued. She shrank back to avoid a soaking freshman who was flinging her long hair like a dog just out of the pool.

Now KC was confused. Why should Courtney be concerned with Winnie? Winnie was as far from sorority material as it was possible to be. Then KC breathed in sharply as she realized that Courtney wasn't talking about Winnie. She was referring to Lauren.

"Lauren is not a girl who should be seen with her clothes plastered to her body," Courtney went on.

KC wanted to defend Lauren. Did everyone have to be physically perfect to be accepted in a sorority? Besides, who was to say which shape was "perfect" and which was not?

"I don't mean to be cruel," Courtney said. "And I didn't say anything to her. I'm sure she didn't even see me. I like you, KC, and I like Lauren. I think you both would make great Tri Betas. Especially you. But I'm in the minority on Lauren. She can't afford slip-ups like this. And you can't afford to share them with her."

KC stood still, shivering and speechless. She'd sensed all along that there might be some Tri Beta resistance to Lauren. But she'd assumed that money and family would cut through all that. "But she got asked to the dream date dance. She's one of the only girls I know that did," KC objected. "I thought that meant she was in for sure."

Courtney looked up in shock. "A fraternity brother asked Lauren Turnbell-Smythe to be his brother's dream date?"

KC wasn't sure what to make of Courtney's alarm. "Mark Geisslinger from ODT asked her."

"He gave her a card, right?"

KC nodded.

"What card?"

"The king of hearts."

"Oh, no." Courtney looked truly pained.

"What? What's wrong?"

"I can't tell you." Courtney lifted her face for a moment, looking like she was about to explain. Then she seemed to change her mind. "It's against house rules. I could be kicked out for telling you."

"You mean it's a prank. Is Lauren being set up with some horrible creep?"

Courtney stood very still. The bathroom was starting to empty out and her silence seemed to have flooded the whole place. "I can't say."

KC felt like she was on the verge of passing out. Lauren trusted her, Maybe she was growing apart from Winnie and even Faith, but they had always trusted each other. They might argue and even criticize one another, but betrayal was a different story. "Shouldn't we warn her? We can't just let Lauren walk into it."

Courtney would no longer look her in the eye. "Oh, yes, we can. We have to. I've told you too much already, and if you say anything to Lauren, you will automatically be ineligible for our house."

"Why?"

"KC, these are the traditions and rituals of rush. If you don't like them, stay in the dorms. And I'll tell you something else. If Lauren makes it in, there will be even more Dream Date Dances, and April Fools' Day Flings and Blind Date Roommate Socials. That's the way it is. Tri Betas are known as the most successful, wealthiest, *and* best-looking girls on campus. If Lauren joins us, she'll keep getting singled out. She has to decide if the house is that important to her, and if she can take it."

"That's horrible. Why even ask her back if you know that?" KC cried out.

Courtney took a deep breath. "Don't be so innocent, KC. Her mother gave our house a huge donation. If Lauren wants to join, we'll probably have to let her in. But that doesn't mean Marielle and the others who don't like her will be any nicer. That's why this kind of test may not be so cruel. It may convince Lauren to drop out on her own."

"Which is just what you and the other sisters

would like." KC caught Courtney's eye, and wondered if she'd gone too far.

But Courtney merely shrugged, examined herself in the mirror, and got ready to leave. "That's for Lauren to decide." Courtney touched KC's hand. "As for you, we need you at the house tonight at six. You'll carry some decorations over to ODT and put them up. Bring your party clothes. You can change in my room. You will be there, won't you?"

KC nodded.

"Good. I'll see you then."

KC stayed in the bathroom long after Courtney had gone, until every freshman girl had returned to the dorms and the restroom felt like a cold, empty, white-tiled cell. She stared at herself in the big mirror. Even under the streaked mascara and the messy hair, she saw a face that looked good. Her face and body impressed people through little effort of her own. Because of that, doors would open to her—with or without an inheritance. She would be spared whatever was going to happen to Lauren.

KC knew that she should get going. She had to wash her hair again, decide on a party dress, make sure she had her waitress gear, and get herself on track. But she already felt guilty and dishonest. She was also beginning to feel tired, dreadfully tired.

What with Winnie, rush, and the sheer lack of sleep from waitressing at night, KC's body was starting to feel deprived of some vital ingredient.

She dragged herself past the sinks, avoiding the mirror this time, and started to walk out. She didn't want to think about Lauren and what was going to happen. She didn't want to think about what Faith and Winnie would say. And she didn't know how many more times she could look herself in the face.

Fifteen

"Come on, Brooks!" Faith yelled, holding out her hand as the wind pushed against her.

Brooks kept running, weaving across the green as if he were chasing a soccer ball. The fierce wind had blown a pink paper flower out of Faith's hand. It was only a silly souvenir from their dinner downtown, but Brooks was going after it as if it were her favorite hat.

Faith's hair whipped across her mouth and eyes. She yelled, "It's not important, Brooks. Let it go!"

"I've almost got it," he yelled back.

Faith looked up at the sky, which was getting

dark and spongy-looking. A big storm was on its way. The wind swirled and blew. Towels flapped out of dorm windows. A sapling had already blown over on the dorm green, and orientation brochures were scattered from the dining commons to the parking lot.

"Brooks, forget it!"

He finally turned back. The wind forced his parka open and blew his scarf off.

Faith laughed. Dinner had been great. No heavy discussions and no big breakthroughs, but no worries, either. Just easy fun. They'd eaten burgers and goofed around, stealing each other's French fries. They'd talked about their families, about Lauren and Barney, and about what was probably happening with their high school friends. It had been almost like old times.

"Got it!" Brooks yelled as he finally caught up with her paper flower. He grabbed it with one hand and, without breaking his stride, circled to get his scarf, then raced back to meet her.

"Victory!" he sang, holding up his two trophies.

Faith grabbed him around the waist and the next minute had tackled him to the ground. His arms swept around her and then they were rolling and laughing.

They looked into each other's faces and sighed.

As they kissed, Faith was aware of wind and hair, skin and grass. The air was getting heavy, and she felt a few drops of rain.

Faith pulled back and smiled at him. "Let's get back to my dorm room."

He helped her up. Huddled together, they slowly crossed the green.

It took both of them to pull Faith's lobby door closed against the strong wind. Inside, a fire was lit in the lobby fireplace. Tap shoes were tapping somewhere on the first floor. Practice scales were lilting up and down. There was the scent of coffee and oil paints.

They climbed the stairs and walked by Kimberly and Freya's room. They and four or five other girls from the floor were huddled around a steaming pizza, chattering and singing along with a musical score coming from Kimberly's tape player.

Faith waved and walked the few feet to her room. She dug in her bag for her key. Her hand shook as she tried to open the door, and for the first time that night she realized that she was nervous. Her stomach had dropped to her toes, and she wondered whether she could go through with her plan. But she smiled back at Brooks and kept fiddling with the lock.

"I'll get it," Brooks said over the chatter and

the music. He took the key from her and managed to open the door.

The room was dark except for the glow of a single desk lamp. Faith feared for a moment that Lauren had come home early, even though she was supposed to spend the night at KC's.

But Lauren wasn't home. The room was a little cold, with a trace of Lauren's expensive perfume clinging to the air. Outside the wind snarled and whistled.

Faith smiled at Brooks as they walked in. Next door's party talk came indistinctly through the wall.

"Here we are," Brooks said, as if he, too, were suddenly nervous.

"Here we are," Faith repeated. After the words came out Faith wondered why she hadn't just blurted *I love you*. Neither of them had ever said those words. Faith couldn't quite get them to her lips even then.

She wound her arms around Brooks's neck and kissed him fiercely, almost roughly.

After the kiss Brooks stared into her eyes. She looked into his face and saw something new there—something strong and loving and brave. At least she hoped she did.

Faith took a deep breath. It was happening. She

was taking the leap, she told herself, changing herself forever.

When Brooks turned away to watch the wind blasting over the dark green, Faith lit a candle that Winnie had given her. Then she took the card that she'd made earlier—the one with a big Z printed across it. Quietly she taped it up and closed her dorm room door.

The ODT fraternity house was anything but quiet. It rocked. It rolled. In the storm it stood out like the final firework on the Fourth of July. Every other frat party looked dead in comparison.

"KC," Lauren whispered to herself, "where are you?"

She stood alone on the windy sidewalk. Even though the wind pushed and prodded her, she stood as if her heels had been planted in the ground. She couldn't move, and she could barely think. As the other partygoers hustled past her, Lauren let the wind assault her face, just to remind herself that she was still alive.

The ODT house was only a hundred yards away. It was a classic Colonial, with four massive columns in front and a bright white door that had been flung wide open. The place was packed. Dancing bodies flashed in the windows. Rushees and active members were bottled up in the entrance, a few even singing. One couple was necking right under the front porch light.

Lauren licked her dry lips and forced herself to swallow. Besides her anxiety about her dream date, she was overwhelmed by the sheer maleness of this party. The Tri Betas were intimidating, but at least they created a feminine environment she could relate to. ODT's head-banging let-it-all-hang-out wildness rushed over her like a stampede. If Lauren had little experience with close female friendships, she had next to none with men.

"Just go," she whispered to herself. "Just move your feet and go."

She made her way to the edge of the ODT lawn, then stood still again while a group of rushees passed her by and hurried to the front door.

Lauren had to wait while the boy at the door checked IDs. She gulped a deep breath of night air and dabbed at her lipstick. The people in front of her went in, and her heart began pounding so hard she thought she might fall over. She fumbled in her pocket, clutching the King of Hearts.

A moment later Lauren stood face to face with the door keeper, whom she immediately recognized as her musical matchmaker, Mark Geisslinger.

"You made it!" he said. Then he leaned toward her and whispered, "The king is waiting."

There was something about Mark that sent chills up Lauren's spine. Praying that she would run into KC, she followed Mark into the house.

If the outside impression of the frat house was different from that of the Tri Beta house, the inside was even more of a departure. Lauren could tell that some of the decorations had been supplied by sorority sisters, but other than that, there wasn't much attention to details. The living room was big and wood-paneled, classy in a dingy way. It looked like a hangout in which guys could drink beer and put up their feet.

Mark took the playing card from Lauren and held it up in the air. Another frat brother blew a shrill metal whistle, and suddenly the noise and dancing came to a halt. Everyone in the ODT living room turned and stared at her.

"Another dream date has just arrived," Mark announced. "This young lady is rushing Tri Beta, and she has the *king of hearts*. Will the king please come forward and claim his dream date?"

For a long moment no one came out of the crowd, and Lauren wanted to die. She knew as well as anyone that she wasn't a frat brat siren. She was prepared for the king of hearts to be a total nerd. But when she looked up again and didn't see *any* frat brother come forward, she wondered if he had taken one look at her and escaped out the back door.

Then there was a parting in the Tri Beta crowd and for a second Lauren spotted KC. KC wouldn't quite look at her, but Lauren couldn't concern herself with that for long. Her eyes were riveted to the person who was heading toward her, holding up the king of hearts and looking over at his roommate with a wry smile.

"Oh," Lauren sighed.

It was Christopher Hammond. Six feet tall, auburn-haired, confident, graceful Christopher. He wore pleated slacks, tailored jacket, and a red striped tie. For a moment everyone stared, then there were a few giggles. But Lauren didn't hear them. All she saw was Christopher taking his place in front of her.

Lauren held out her playing card. Her hand was shaking so fiercely that he could barely take it from her. Christopher looked back at Mark Geisslinger, who was standing against the refreshment table. Then Christopher took another king of hearts from his jacket pocket and handed it to her. There was some applause, whispers, and more laughter.

For a split second Lauren thought, here it comes, the pie in the face, the spit in the eye. *God help me, take me away from here. Let me close my eyes and simply disappear. Let me back at the hotel with my mother. Anything but this.*

But nothing happened.

Christopher took a deep breath and stood tall. He smiled and held out his hand. "Your name again?" he asked. "I'm sorry. I can't remember."

Lauren could barely speak. "Lauren. Lauren Turnbell-Smythe."

He didn't repeat his name. Of course not. No one forgot the name of a person like Christopher. And yet there was gentleness in his face, his wonderful, classy, fabulous face.

"Well, Lauren," he said in a friendly voice. "It looks like you're my dream date."

Lauren gazed up at him again, unable to take her eyes off his square jaw and his sparkling white smile.

Christopher glanced back once more at Mark and then said gallantly, "Would you like to dance?"

Lauren clung to his arm, breathed in his heady cologne, and floated with him onto the dance floor.

Sixteen

"Party dorm," Winnie muttered as she limped to Forest Hall and heard the insistent thump of Led Zeppelin. "Give me a break." She glared into the dorm lobby. The scene was almost as wild as it had been at the toga party.

She had just returned from a late evening jog. Since it was so windy, she'd been literally running in circles on a track inside the university gym. Her legs were tired. Her head felt like an old tin can. Her memory was rusty and her heart was sore.

"Just go back to your room and sleep," Winnie told herself, holding her head down and moving through the noisy, hopping lobby. "Don't think about anything now. Don't think about Josh. Don't think about KC. Don't think about what a stupid jerk you are. Just get some rest."

But all she could think was, why was she such an idiot? If she was so smart, then why did she always act so dumb? All she wanted was to be the girl who had zip and wildness, who was different and carefree. And all she ended up doing was acting like a ridiculous fool.

She saw something that made her throat clutch. Josh was sitting on the lobby sofa with an Asian guy that Winnie hadn't seen before. They were having an intense conversation.

Winnie wondered if the Asian guy was Josh's new roommate. She told herself to walk up to them and introduce herself, to act like everything was just fine. But she couldn't do it. She doubted she would be able to walk through the Forest lobby ever again.

"So what am I supposed to do?" she asked out loud.

If she couldn't face Josh, how was she supposed to get to her room? "Coed dorms," she swore.

Winnie was beginning to realize just what the concept of "coed dorm" really meant. In high school, if she liked someone but made a fool of herself over him, she might have to see him in class. She might even have to play him in volleyball or sit next to him on the bus. But here! Every morning until June she might run into Josh in the hall. She'd know when he had other girlfriends. She might see Josh every night before she went to bed or every time she went downstairs to get a candy bar. Every time she breathed.

The more she thought running into him, the more sure Winnie was that she couldn't look Josh in the face. Not that night, and maybe not ever.

Finally Winnie retreated. She walked around the back of the dorm until she found the emergency exit. She prayed that an alarm wouldn't go off as she opened it. After all that had gone wrong that week, it wouldn't have surprised her. But nothing happened.

Winnie rushed through the basement, past the candy machines and video games, the study room, the mailboxes, and the ping pong table. She had just stepped into the back stairwell when she heard the splat of water and male voices echoing from above.

"Bombs away!"

"Heads up!"

Water balloons were suddenly flying from above, exploding on the concrete stairs and off the walls. One burst just over Winnie's head and she let the water drip down her face, where it mixed with her tears.

"Stop," she muttered. "Please, stop." All she wanted was to get to her room!

But as soon as she made it to the hallway outside her room, she saw someone that made her feel even more besieged.

"Melissa," Winnie murmured.

Melissa was just leaving the shower, toweling her red hair and shuffling down the hall.

Melissa turned, as if she'd known that Winnie was standing there, but she didn't say anything. She took one look at Winnie, then let herself into their room, slamming the door behind her with a hollow, angry whack.

Winnie stared blearily down the hall until she heard the water ballooners making their way back up the stairs. Before they had a chance to ambush her again, Winnie raced past them and into the bathroom. There she stayed, tears streaming down her face, sitting in the shower with her running clothes still on and the water blasting down.

KC was chatting with Courtney at the ODT house.

"Of course we consider appearance and background when we invite girls to join our house," Courtney was telling her.

KC nodded.

"But we also look for an inner quality."

"Oh, yes. Of course."

They were in the ODT dining room. There were almost as many members and rushees in there as there were out on the dance floor.

"We look for a certain something," Courtney continued. "It's hard to describe. Personality. Character. We really do. At least, I look for those things."

"I know you do."

Courtney glanced at her nearby sorority sister, Marielle, who was perched on a counter, eating chips and jangling her charm bracelet. Five Tri Beta rushees surrounded Marielle, hanging on her every twangy word and laughing adoringly.

Courtney sighed as she watched Marielle. "Still, sometimes girls who aren't really very nice get in. But that isn't our intention."

KC kept nodding, as if her head were on a string. She had been tagging along with Courtney all evening, refilling the punch bowl, helping Courtney keep track of which girls were there and who had been picked out as dream dates. Courtney wasn't merely tolerating KC; she seemed to have taken KC under her wing.

"So next is the big interview, and then you make your final selections?" KC asked as she glanced around. The last time she'd spotted Lauren, Lauren had been starting her second dance with Christopher. He'd looked pleasant, if a little bored, while Lauren moved in his arms with dreamy grace.

Courtney nodded. "Tomorrow night, the final group of rushees will each have an individual interview before the whole house. Don't worry. I've talked to most of the girls about you. Everyone agrees you're up to Tri Beta standards. And now you've proved your loyalty by not warning your friend, Lauren, about the dream date prank."

"Yes." KC swallowed back her shame. Courtney's attention was so flattering and so heady that once KC had seen Lauren and Christopher dancing together, she'd pushed away any guilt about what kind of trap had been set for her vulnerable new friend.

Courtney smoothed her hair. "On Sunday you find out who made the last cut." She sighed. "That's the really bloody one. But you'll make it. Still, I'll be glad when rush is over. I try to be decent and kind during rush, but there are parts of it that are cruel no matter what."

KC knew Courtney was referring to Lauren again. She still didn't know exactly what kind of prank had been played on Lauren, and she was hoping that she never would know. She prayed it would turn out to be something so subtle and sophisticated that Lauren could go back to her dorm room later that night not knowing, either. But then the music stopped. There was a split second of silence, in which KC heard Marielle's energetic, twangy voice.

"Attention, everyone," Marielle began in a stage whisper. She was talking to her group of five Tri Beta rushees. "An important rush secret is about to be divulged. For those new rushees who don't already know, and that should be most of you," she said with a chuckle, "the dream date tradition is a test, and it works two ways. There are real dream dates, girls who are the most gorgeous humans in all of rush." She glanced around the room. "But there's another name for this dance, too."

"What's that?"

"I figured there was something weird going on."

"Some of you are perceptive." Marielle smiled with pleasure. "This is also the traditional Trash Your Roommate dance."

"The what?"

"Trash your roommate. If you're a knockout, then you're really a dream date. But if you were asked out by your date's roommate and you're *not* a knockout, then . . ."

Five palms went to five mouths at once.

"Oh, no!"

"How humiliating."

"I'd never show my face again. Never!"

"How do you know which you are?"

Marielle went on. "It's very easy. If some incredible guy is fixed up with a doggy rushee, then it's pretty clear who's trash and who's dreaming if they think it's a dream date."

Courtney had started to inch away, but KC caught her, grabbing her silk sleeve. "So that's it?"

Courtney would barely look at her.

"Lauren is the worst date Mark Geisslinger could find for his roommate?"

Courtney wouldn't answer.

"Tell me," KC demanded. "Was Lauren asked to be Christopher's date as some kind of horrible rush joke?"

Courtney answered with a single, uncomfortable nod.

KC knew that Marielle and her admirers were discussing the same topic. They were gloating smarmily, and couldn't help chattering at the same time.

"If you ask me, I thought Christopher acted with admirable restraint."

"He was so nice about it, it's disgusting."

"She's *only* twenty pounds overweight."

"Talk about trashed."

"But not even trashy. Just plain dull."

"Really. But what a guy he is."

"What a hunk."

"What a doll."

Meanwhile KC was getting dizzy, and her entire body was breaking into a sweat. The girls around her kept up their chattering, buzzing blur, like a swarm of overdressed, overperfumed bees. The only face KC could focus on was Courtney's.

There was a sadness in Courtney's eyes. KC began to wonder if Courtney didn't feel a little shame and guilt, too. She thought back to Lauren's Cinderella expression and felt even sicker. "Does Lauren know? Will she know?"

Courtney shrugged. "Actually, she's had it easy so far."

"How can you say that?"

"Look, KC, Christopher is a lot nicer than most guys who have been in his position. He's one of the most desirable guys on campus. I bet he'll be a big television producer some day. I've seen ordinary frat brothers laugh in a girl's face at the Trash Your Roommate dance. I've seen them tear their playing cards in little pieces in front of everyone and then lead their dates outside to the dumpster."

"Oh, my God. Will Lauren find out?"

Courtney pulled herself together. "KC, she'd be a fool if she hasn't figured it out by now. So you see why it's best for her to drop out of rush. If she doesn't, we'll have to ask her back for the final interview because of her mother. And she'll feel even more humiliated."

KC was surprised at her reaction. No matter how much she wanted to be a Tri Beta, she couldn't stomach this. "Why didn't you let me tell her? Why didn't I just tell her on my own?"

"Don't let this change your mind about joining us," Courtney warned her. "I know it's cruel, but life is cruel. You're not in high school anymore, KC. The whole reason our sorority is so desirable is because we turn so many girls away. If we took every girl that came along, then being accepted by us wouldn't mean a thing."

KC told herself that Courtney was right. If she wanted to get ahead, she couldn't crumble under her very first test. But when she turned to talk to Courtney again, she realized that Courtney was no longer standing next to her. Someone else was. Someone smaller and heavier—someone who was red-eyed and very distraught.

It was Lauren.

"Are you all right?" KC asked awkwardly.

"KC," Lauren managed. "Oh, God."

KC looked into Lauren's violet eyes and saw two wells of humiliation and despair.

Lauren put her hand to her mouth, then to her eyes, her forehead, and her chest. "So I'm the trash," Lauren gasped.

KC pretended innocence. "What?"

"Me."

"What do you mean?"

"Oh, my God. How can I ever face anyone again? And you knew. *You knew!*"

KC went dead inside.

"Why didn't you tell me?" Lauren demanded.

KC had no answer.

"I never should have come to school here." Lauren's eyes overflowed with tears. "I never should have moved into the dorms. I never should have trusted you. Never."

KC had begun to tremble, too. "Why do you blame me?"

Lauren wrung her hands in grief and spoke in a sobbing rush. "You knew! You knew this would happen, and you didn't tell me. Now everyone knows. How can I ever show my face here again?"

"I didn't know all of it!" KC argued. "I didn't know it would be this bad. And even if I had known, I wouldn't have been able to tell you."

"Why? *Why?*"

KC couldn't answer; she no longer knew. Courtney's reasoning would no longer fit inside her brain. How far would she have gone to get into the Tri Betas? To make her contacts for the future? And once she'd made those contacts, how far would she go then? Would she have betrayed Winnie? What about Faith?

Suddenly it was important that Lauren understand why KC had hurt her, why she had gotten so carried away.

But Lauren didn't give KC the chance to explain. "I have to get out of here," she sobbed.

Lauren put her hand up to her face and pushed her way through the rest of the whispering rushees. The sisters and the members of ODT were all staring at her. The last person Lauren passed was Christopher, and then she was gone. KC heard the other girls chattering about what had just happened, making jokes and laughing.

Shut up, all of you! KC wanted to yell. *You're all just feeling good because it didn't happen to you.*

But KC suddenly realized that she'd been feeling so good for exactly the same reason: because she knew so many of the other girls were going to be rejected and ruined, while she would rise above them and succeed. Unable to look anyone in the face, she, too, pushed her way out of the crowd.

Seventeen

Lauren was trying to sneak past the party in Kimberly and Freya's room.

It wasn't going to be easy, considering the way she looked. Her eyes were swollen, red, and ringed in smudged makeup. She moved haltingly, as if she were wounded. And she knew that if anyone so much as looked at her, she would break down again.

She barely remembered making it back to Coleridge. Her walk back had been a windy, rambling blur. What did stick in Lauren's mind was the guilty look on KC's face, the horrible tittering of the girls, and the bland warmth in Christopher's eyes that she'd taken for affection but later realized was only pity. Recalling any one of those memories made Lauren want to crawl back to her mother and never trust anyone ever again.

Lauren had only made it to the lavatory door when she froze, overhearing the party chit-chat spilling out of Kimberly and Freya's open door.

"Okay," Freya was announcing. "Everybody has to sing their favorite song about falling in love."

"No!" cried half a dozen voices.

"Yes!" Kimberly agreed. "I'm a dancer, but I'll sing if everyone else does. I heard Professor Cohen makes everyone do this on the first day of his music performance class. Come on."

A few days earlier Lauren would have given anything to be friends with Kimberly and the other girls on her floor. But as she stood there she never wanted to think about friends again.

"How could she do it?" Lauren whispered. Silent tears streamed down her face. As crushed as she was over Christopher, as humiliated as the sorority girls had made her feel, that still wasn't the worst. It was KC's behavior that was the hardest to swallow—the fact that her supposed new friend had seen the whole horrible thing coming and hadn't lifted a finger to stop it. Lauren had trusted someone for once, and it had all blown up right in her face.

The chatter in Kimberly and Freya's room had

leveled to a continuous, giggly hum, and Lauren decided it was time to move. She hurried past the open door and made it to her room unnoticed. But then she froze again. She wasn't sure if she could face Faith. After all, Faith was one of KC's best friends.

And then she saw the card on the door. The index card with the big Z on it. Of course. Faith had planned a big romantic evening with Brooks. When Lauren thought about Faith and Brooks being so much in love, it only made her feel like more of a misfit.

"I don't belong here, and I never will," Lauren muttered as she hurried past Kimberly and Freya's room again and ran back down the hall.

"Lauren!" Kimberly called out.

Lauren didn't slow down. She was finally grateful for the new BMW her mother had bought her and delivered to the dorm parking lot.

Barely thinking, she ran out of the dorm, across the green, and into the parking lot. She got into her car, slammed the door, and began to drive.

"Even for me, this is a new low."

Winnie was still in the shower stall. She'd turned the faucet off and was just sitting there, shivering, feeling the occasional vibration from the party going on downstairs. Her tights and sweatshirt felt like cold mud against her skin.

"Welcome to college," she muttered.

She stood up, stomping water out of her shoes. Then she put her forehead against the cold, wet tile and tried to figure out what she was going to do next.

"Melissa, why don't you just disappear?" Winnie whispered. "Why don't you and Josh and KC and every other freshman at this dumb school just take a hike?"

It was bad enough remembering what a fool she'd been with Josh. It was even worse to think that she'd ruined her friendship with KC. But at that moment, the worst part of her messy freshman life was Melissa. If she couldn't face her roommate again, what was she going to do? Stay in the shower forever? Sleep on the roof?

Winnie got out of the stall, blotted her hair and clothes with paper towels, then steeled herself to go back through the hallway. She knew she might run into Josh, but she had no choice.

The hall was empty. Winnie raced down, squishing in her shoes and leaving a trail of water. Quickly, she opened her door.

"Hello," she said.

Melissa was sitting at her desk. She looked at

Winnie, then went back to her fat textbook, as if Winnie weren't even there.

"Same to you," Winnie muttered. She grabbed her towel from the hook on the door, then picked her way through the underwear, tapes, and makeup containers that formed a landscape around her bed. After drying her hair, she threw her clothes in the bottom of her closet, put the makeup in one of her carpetbags, and stacked the tapes on the shelf above her desk. Even though Melissa kept staring at her book, Winnie sensed that her roommate was paying attention to her. Melissa hadn't turned the page in a very long time.

"So I'm a slob," Winnie finally offered.

Melissa didn't move.

"I'm not a murderer, you know."

Melissa closed her book.

Winnie peeled off her wet gym clothes and put on dry leotards and an oversized man's jacket.

Melissa turned to look at her, and Winnie stared back. She saw a determined, almost tough-looking girl with red hair and pale, freckled skin. "Look, I'm sorry about taking your sheet."

When Melissa still didn't say anything, Winnie began to chatter. "I'll try to clean up my stuff, okay? If something really bugs you, you can just tell me. You know, write me a note, send me a telegram, whatever. I know I woke you up the other night when I came in so late—or early—but you don't have to act like I'm the Wicked Witch of the West. I didn't *mean* to wake you up. It's just orientation week. How was I supposed to know you were such a light sleeper?"

Melissa still didn't respond.

Finally, Winnie talked back to herself. "Winnie, shut up for once. Just transfer to another dorm. Get another roommate. This is hopeless." She turned her back on Melissa, put on her duck boots and started combing out her hair.

That was when Winnie heard Melissa speak up. "Is it raining out?"

Winnie almost dropped her comb. "What?"

Melissa had turned in her chair. "Has it started to rain? It sounded like the wind was dying down." She shrugged. "Of course, who can hear anything in this dorm?"

"No, it's not raining."

Melissa looked a little confused, and glanced at Winnie's wet hair and pile of soggy clothes.

Winnie stood up, slapping her hands together. She almost went into another monologue, but for once she decided to keep things to herself. She simply said, "I'll tell you about it sometime, if you're interested."

While the party rumbled and throbbed downstairs, Winnie and Melissa looked at each other.

"So can we start over?" Winnie asked tentatively. She suddenly wished she could start the whole thing over—orientation, college, Josh, her friendship with KC. "I know I can't undo being a slob and waking you up, but we really don't know each other yet, so maybe it's a little early to decide it won't work out."

Melissa nodded and gradually began to smile.

Winnie started to feel a little calmer. She was beginning to realize that throwing herself into things wasn't always such a good idea. Maybe the early, slower, getting-to-know-you parts were more important than she'd realized.

"I'm sorry, too," Melissa admitted. "I wasn't so much mad at you as I am at this whole noisy dorm."

The music from the lobby party shook the walls once more.

"Tell me about it."

They both laughed.

Winnie stuck her hands in her pockets. She was starting to feel a little more patient, a little braver. She was glad she hadn't avoided Melissa. Maybe she still didn't have the courage to face Josh, but she wondered if there was any possibility of making up with KC. "Listen, I think this party's going to be rocking and rolling for a while longer.

I could sure use a cup of coffee. And I know a place off campus that's always open late."

Melissa stood up. "I don't drink coffee. But I could use some fresh air. How about if I walk you across the green and we can talk?"

"All right. Let's go." Winnie buttoned up her jacket, then turned out the light and followed Melissa out the door.

Eighteen

"It's Friday night," KC muttered. "You'd think there'd be more customers."

The Beanery was very quiet. Practically the only sounds were the folk singer strumming his guitar and the hiss of steam from the espresso machine. There were a few customers but not enough to keep KC busy, not enough to keep her from thinking about everything that had happened.

When she'd gotten to work, KC had gone to the employees' locker room and stripped off the dress she'd bought with Lauren's credit card. After that she had put on the wrap skirt her mother had given her, a pair of tennis shoes, her Beanery T-shirt, and her old waitress apron from her parents' restaurant with Trust Our Ingredients printed across the front. Then she'd worked like a crazy person, stacking dishes, refilling sugar bowls, folding napkins, and setting tables for the morning shift. If a Tri Beta showed up, she wouldn't have time to talk. If an ODT brother came in, she might not even know.

But all her chores were finished, and the place was quiet. There was nothing to do but stand and think about what she'd done.

Out of the corner of her eye KC saw a couple sit down. She picked up a damp rag and went over.

"How are you tonight?" she recited emptily, not bothering to look at their faces. She wiped every inch of the table and picked up her tip from the previous pair.

"You missed a spot," said a twangy female voice.

"What?"

The customer pointed with a long red nail. "You missed a spot. Right there. What is that? Gross."

KC automatically rubbed harder, until she finally looked up and recognized them. It was Marielle, from Tri Beta, and Christopher's roommate, Mark Geisslinger. One look at their smug, handsome faces brought it all back—a landslide of guilt and regret.

KC gritted her teeth. "What can I get for you?"

Marielle recognized her, too. "Oh, Mark, this is

KC. She's a rushee—a friend of that, uh, plump girl with all the money." She grabbed Mark's hand. "Did you see Chris's face when you announced his dream date?" Both Marielle and Mark started to howl, then looked back up at KC and stifled their laughter. "You know, I never found out what KC stands for. Kind and Clever, or something like that, right?"

"Actually it stands for Kahia Cayanne."

"What?" Mark guffawed.

KC didn't repeat it.

"Did you know, KC," Marielle said, putting her red nails to her cheek, "from this night until the end of rush you're not allowed to speak to a sorority sister outside of the house? That rule starts at—" she checked her watch "—midnight tonight. So you're already in trouble."

There were so many rush rules and traditions, KC didn't know how any one person could keep track of them. She stared down at her pad and said nothing.

Marielle grinned. "So. I'd like an iced cappuccino, but I want it made special."

Mark tittered.

"I want it with a half-teaspoon of chocolate syrup added—no more, no less. And I don't want you to use hot coffee, so all the ice melts. Just to make sure, I want an extra single cube of ice. On the side. And I want an extra cookie." Marielle leaned back. "Did you get all that down?"

Swallowing her anger, KC nodded, took Mark's order and went back to the kitchen.

"You have to do this," KC convinced herself as she made up the order. "It's no big deal." She put Marielle's iced cappuccino on her little round tray. The half teaspoon of syrup was included, and she placed two cookies on the napkin beside the coffee. There was a huckleberry malt for Mark. And the single cube of ice was skating around on a butter dish.

KC told herself it was nothing but a rush test, a little bit of hazing. Compared to what Lauren had been through, it was the most innocent of jokes.

Clutching the sides of her tray, KC carried it out to the floor. When she got to the table she glanced back at the front door, just to see whether someone needed to be seated. Someone was there, but it wasn't whom KC had been expecting. It wasn't a rushee winding down after a frat party, nor a couple out on a Friday night date.

It was Winnie.

She looked surprisingly calm. Her hair was damp, and she wasn't wearing makeup. She just stood there in a big, dark jacket, a few feet from the cash register, looking around the room.

When Winnie's eyes met KC's, she smiled hesitantly. And that was when KC's feeling came back. She wanted Winnie to run over and hug her, to jump up and down and wave the way Winnie would have done a week earlier. KC wanted to share Winnie's intensity, her warmth and her sense of fun.

Carrying her tray, KC made a detour over to the door. But as soon as she approached, Winnie became defensive. "Look, KC, it's been a very weird night, and I need a cup of coffee. Don't worry. I won't let anyone know that I'm your friend. Or rather, *was* your friend."

KC wasn't sure what to say. Had she treated Winnie so badly that they weren't even friends anymore? KC wanted to explain things to Winnie. She wanted to say, *I remember you coming over at midnight last spring to cheer me up after I wasn't picked as Most Likely to Succeed. I remember how much I missed you over the summer and how jealous I was that you got to go so far away. Maybe I was too impressed by the Tri Betas. Maybe I put too much importance on Lauren's background and her wealth, and too little on her heart.*

But KC didn't say anything, because Winnie walked right by her. Quiet for once in her life, Winnie sat down at the table next to Marielle and Mark, picked up a menu, and stared down at it.

KC looked back down at her tray. The single

cube of ice was melting, and for all she knew, Marielle would send it back and make her bring another. Staring down at that slippery cube, KC's anger at the Tri Betas began to return in full force. As she approached Marielle's table, she was becoming so furious that she didn't know what to do.

"Here's your cappuccino and your malt," she said.

Marielle had been whispering something to Mark. She looked annoyed at KC's interruption. "I told you, KC," she warned, "you're not allowed to talk to me. I'm going to have to tell Courtney. Now, not another word out of you."

"I'm so sorry." KC managed. She couldn't resist adding, "Oops, that was a word, wasn't it? Three words, actually."

"KC," Marielle barked, "I'm serious. This is rush. I wouldn't fool around if I were you. It's bad enough that you hung out with Lauren for so long."

Mark watched in amusement.

"I'm *not* fooling around," KC shot back. "As a matter of fact, I've never been more serious."

"And what is that supposed to mean?"

KC looked back over at Winnie, who had put down her menu and was watching with interest. Suddenly KC knew that her old friendship was on the line. She hadn't done it for Lauren, but maybe she could still do it for Winnie. She could do it for herself.

"What are you waiting for, KC?" Marielle demanded.

"You can put my malt right here," said Mark, pushing aside a napkin and opening his arms.

"Anything you say," KC responded with a smile.

"Be careful. What are you doing?"

"Oh, no!" KC sang happily. "I'm *sooooooooo* sorry."

"What are you doing?"

While Winnie watched open-mouthed and Marielle screamed, KC took the cup of iced cappuccino, the malt, and the single cube of ice, and dumped them over Mark and Marielle.

"I'm so, so sorry," KC said again as the trail of ice cream and coffee oozed down Mark and Marielle and started dripping on the floor.

KC looked at Winnie again and gave her a very big smile.

It was happening almost the way Faith had imagined it.

She and Brooks were slow dancing in her barely lit dorm room. Moonlight filtered in, and Winnie's candle gave off a sweet scent. The tree outside the window rustled. They could hear muffled giggles from Freya and Kimberly's get-together next door.

Faith and Brooks were close, her arms around his neck and his around her waist. They were swaying just a little, every once in a while taking a tiny step. Brooks's curls were soft against the side of her face, and her long hair flowed over his shoulder. She could almost feel the soothing beat of his heart. She dropped one of her hands and slid it under his sweater, touching his smooth, bare back.

Then they were kissing. Short kisses first, leading to longer ones that nearly made Faith reel. She was nearly dizzy. Nearly happy.

Yet Faith was aware that there was something missing.

"I haven't stepped on your feet," she joked.

"Not yet," Brooks said solemnly.

Faith hadn't said anything about what she'd planned, because she hadn't known how to say it. Or if it was even something people talked about at all. But she sensed that it wasn't supposed to happen like this. Although they danced, the music didn't move her. Although she felt Brooks breathe, she couldn't help paying attention to the party going on next door. Although they held each other, she worried about what was going to happen next.

Brooks dipped her in his corny tango move. Faith kissed him and even as their mouths touched, she was wondering what was wrong. Everything felt out of kilter, but she couldn't pin down the reason. Every time Faith touched or kissed Brooks, she felt as if she were watching herself, as if she were doing a love scene for a movie camera. Her heart didn't seem to be connected to her lips or her arms.

Faith started to sing along with the music, which she hoped would make Brooks laugh, since she was a terrible singer. Their relationship had always been at its best when they could be playful. But Brooks didn't seem to notice and kept on dancing. Finally Faith intentionally stepped on his toes, which started a foot fight that ended with them both toppling back onto her bed.

"Gotcha," she said.

Brooks smiled.

They sat on the edge of the narrow mattress. There was a lull in the party next door, and for a moment it was totally quiet. Faith had a strange, nervous feeling as she clasped her hands in front of her. She and Brooks were sitting like two strangers. Faith wasn't sure quite what was going wrong or how she should proceed.

"Brooks," she finally said.

"Yes?" He seemed preoccupied, too.

Faith leaned her head on his shoulder, but she didn't fall back onto the bed or try to kiss him again. It occurred to her what a huge step it was that she was trying to take.

"Did you want to tell me something?" Brooks asked. He rubbed his hand over his face and seemed a little tired.

"What?"

"This morning you said you wanted to talk. Was there something special you wanted to say?"

"I'm not sure."

"Faith." He leaned closer. "You said that was the whole reason you wanted to get together tonight. That you had to talk to me about something. Don't you remember?"

What was Faith supposed to do? Come right out and say it? Her imagination had skipped over this part. She'd thought it would be just like a scene in the movies: kiss, fall back on the bed, fade out. Cut. Morning. She'd figured that the in between part just happened naturally. But this wasn't feeling natural at all.

"What was it?"

Faith couldn't say anything, because she was beginning to figure out what was really on her mind. Something like, *Well, Brooks, actually my plan was to invite you back here and seduce you. I wanted our relationship to be different, to be closer. But this feels so awkward that I'm beginning to wonder if we should have been closer a long time ago.*

After another pause, Brooks took her hand. "Okay, Faith. I know you were mad when I wouldn't leave the climbing rock. And I know something was going on the night of the toga party. All this college stuff is a lot to deal with. But don't worry. Everything will be okay."

"How do you know?" she asked.

"How do I know what?"

"That everything will be okay."

"I'll make it okay," he said with a decisive nod.

Faith stiffened. "Brooks, whatever you do, you can't make everything okay for *me*."

Brooks became tense, too. "Are you still mad because I put down that assistant directing thing? It wasn't my fault that you didn't drop off your resume."

Faith was stunned by Brooks's change of subject. She stared at him.

"Maybe I should have been more supportive about it," he reconsidered. "But you're only a freshman. I didn't want you to be disappointed."

"That's not it," Faith said, although she began to wonder if that could be it, or a large part of it.

Faith looked at Brooks. She cared so much for him. Maybe she even loved him in an old-friend kind of way. She'd thought of him as her bridge between old and new, but she was beginning to wonder if he weren't a roadblock. She looked around her room at the old stuffed bear, the new book bag. She'd always been one to make new friends and keep the old, but for the first time in her life the old and the new were just not linking up.

"There's plenty of time for you to get involved in the drama department," Brooks went on. "Besides, I get along with most everybody, and I still don't feel very comfortable around those artsy people."

"I do."

"What is that supposed to mean?"

"Brooks," Faith blurted suddenly, unable to stop herself, "do you ever feel that maybe we've been together so long, we don't know why we're together anymore?"

"What?"

What was happening was the opposite of what she'd planned. There had been no romantic rehearsal for this. It was an unstoppable impulse.

"What do you mean?" Brooks's mouth was starting to tremble, and there was a defensive edge to his voice.

Faith looked him right in the eye. "Sometimes I think about how we were when we got together. And then I realize that we're in college now and everything between us is the same as it's been for the last four years!"

"Faith, what are you saying?"

Faith was figuring it out as she went along. She wasn't sure where she was going, only that she had to get there. "I mean, we've known each other since we were kids. We're not kids anymore. I want to grow up, Brooks."

"So?"

Faith stared at him.

His face grew hard. "You think I'm holding you back." The pale moonlight made Brooks's features look like stone.

"No." Faith stood up, put her hands to her head, and began to pace. "I'm holding myself back."

"What do you mean, Faith?"

"Oh, Brooks, I'm probably crazy. You're a wonderful person. I don't know what I mean."

"Yes, you do. You obviously know," he spat out. "Why don't you just come out and say it?"

Faith's thoughts were coming together so fast that she barely knew what she was going to say until it was out of her mouth. "I'm trying."

She thought back to her plans for the night and how ridiculous they all seemed now. Making love wasn't what she wanted. Being closer wasn't what she wanted. No. What she *really* wanted was something else altogether.

"What you're trying to tell me is that you want

to break up," he finally said, sounding empty and hurt.

"What?" Faith gasped. She froze, as if what he'd said was outrageous. But a moment later, when the shock of his words had worn off, she managed to answer, "No. Maybe. God, Brooks, I don't know."

"Yes, you *do*," He stood up, too. "You've known all evening. You knew this morning and that's what you wanted to tell me. Maybe you've known for a really long time." He shook his head. "But you sure picked a weird time to do it." He moved away from her, his mouth tight and his eyes cast down. He looked like a stranger.

"I didn't pick this moment, Brooks. I . . . it just happened."

He paced the room a few times, then bolted for the door. "Well, I'm sorry. Whatever it is that I've done, I'm sorry. You know, all this college stuff isn't exactly easy for me, either!"

"I know. Why should it be easy?" Faith blocked his way. "This isn't your fault!" She wanted to tell him everything, but there was still too much she didn't understand. She wanted to explain that this whole thing didn't have a lot to do with him. It mostly had to do with her. "Brooks, I didn't mean to spring this on you. You know I'm not like that."

"I don't know what you're like anymore."

Before Faith could say another word, he walked out of her dorm room, out of her life. The door slammed.

"I'm not sure I know what I'm like, either," Faith whispered after he was gone. She felt a terrible emptiness, but also a tiny gleam of courage. "All I know is that I have to find out."

Nineteen

After finishing her coffee, Winnie hung out in The Beanery's ladies' room, wondering where the restaurant owner had taken KC for their "talk" and how long it would last. She didn't have to wait long. The bathroom door soon flew open and KC strode in.

Winnie watched her. KC looked upset.

"Hi."

"Hi."

They stood side by side at the mirror, meeting each other's eyes in the glass. There was a sense of being two strangers, and at the same time knowing each other so well that normal conversation wasn't needed.

"You okay?" Winnie asked.

"I'm okay."

"So what'd he say?"

"Who?"

"Your boss, KC. What did he say?"

KC shrugged.

"Did he fire you?"

"I didn't want to keep working after classes started, anyway."

"I guess not."

KC leaned over the sink and let out a big, angry groan. "He told me to leave right now. He doesn't even want me to finish my shift. It seems that even at The Beanery, dumping drinks on customers isn't considered good business practice."

"I see."

"Yeah."

KC stared at herself for a long time in the mirror, then touched her reflection with her fingertips. "I guess I won't have any extra money for clothes. But then again, I won't be going to all those fancy sorority parties."

"You won't?"

"I won't."

Winnie played with her earrings. "If you change

your mind, I could always loan you something of mine."

KC smiled. "Your sweater with the dancing pigs on it."

"My zebra tights."

"Those earrings you used to wear in high school. The ones that looked like pizzas."

"They *were* pizzas. Pepperoni pizzas." Winnie cocked her head. "My boxer shorts. They'd look great on you, too."

"Gee, thanks."

"It's nothing. I'm a generous person."

"I know."

"You do?"

KC nodded. "You're lots of things, Win."

"Yeah. Immature. Pushy. Scared."

"Fun. Smart. Original. Patient with ambitious old friends who lose their heads as soon as they get to college."

"That, too."

They locked eyes and smiled.

Winnie turned her back to the sink, then hopped up to sit on the basin. She swung her feet. "So you really think you'll be rejected by the Tri Betas after what you just did?"

"I'd say my sorority days are definitely over. As a matter of fact, I'm sure of it."

"That's too bad."

"No, it's not," KC said.

"Are you sure?"

KC took a deep, shaky breath. "Yes."

"But I thought that was what you wanted," Winnie said, testing her. "I thought the Tri Betas were all that mattered to you."

KC turned and looked at her. "I changed my mind. I guess I made a mistake. They set up Lauren for an awful prank. I knew something was going to happen, and I didn't stop it."

"Oh, no!"

"Oh, yes. I wish I was brave like you, Win. But I'm not. I just stood there and let it happen."

"I'm not brave."

"I sort of messed up, didn't I, Win?"

"Don't be too hard on yourself." Winnie reached out and hugged her. "We all mess up."

"Yeah. I guess we do."

Winnie didn't say anything else for a while. They were deciding what they wanted to do next when the bathroom door swung open. In walked someone else who looked worn out, scattered, and confused.

"Faith!" the two girls said, running over to their friend.

"I'm so glad you're both here," Faith said. She threw herself in KC and Winnie's arms and hugged them as hard as she could.

* * *

The sleeve of Faith's shirt was torn. A thin scratch ran across her cheek. Still, she felt a little calmer once they'd left The Beanery and gone over to Luigi's for pizza. They sat down in the restaurant. Faith leaned over the checkered tablecloth and shook her head. Her eyes were swollen. Yet her voice was no longer shaking. "I still can't believe it. I can't believe that Brooks and I aren't together anymore."

"Actually, I'm not all that surprised," Winnie said. "I mean I'm a little surprised, but I think it's okay."

"It has to be." Faith sighed. "All I know is that it's time for all of us to meet new people. To do new things."

KC nodded. "As long as we don't cut ourselves off from everything that's old."

Winnie smiled.

They sat for a while picking at the pizza Winnie had ordered: one-third extra cheese for Faith, one-third sausage for KC, and one-third pineapple, onion, and pepperoni for Winnie.

"I don't know what I would have done if I hadn't found you two," Faith said finally, beginning to smile. "It's been such a strange night."

"You can say that again."

"It's been such a strange night."

"Thanks, Win." Faith looked around, as if she were searching for something important. "Do you know how I got out of my room?"

KC and Winnie shook their heads.

"After Brooks left, I climbed down the tree outside my window," Faith explained, as if she couldn't quite believe it herself. "I pried off my window screen and climbed out onto the branch. I almost fell, but I had to get down the trunk. When I finally dropped I almost rolled right into a rose bush. Why did I do that?"

"I don't know. Why did you?" KC asked.

Tangled hair hung down the sides of Faith's pale face. "All of a sudden I'm doing such crazy things. I climbed down the tree because I didn't want to deal with the girls next door. It's strange to think that everyone on your floor practically knows your whole life."

"Welcome to the world of dorms," said Winnie.

Faith held up her hand. Her palm was dirty and scraped. "So I went to both your dorms, and Melissa told me that Winnie was at The Beanery and I remembered that you'd be working, KC."

KC and Winnie nodded.

"And the whole time," Faith said, "I kept wondering why it took me so long to figure out that I didn't belong with Brooks. How could I have convinced myself that everything between us was so great?"

"The same way I convinced myself that everything about the Tri Beta sorority was great," said KC.

"Just like I tried to convince you that everything in my life was great," chimed in Winnie.

Faith and KC gave Winnie puzzled looks, and soon it was all out in the open: the truth about Josh and the toga party, and about Travis and Winnie's summer in France, Faith's plans for her date with Brooks, Lauren and the dream date dance, and KC dumping drinks on Mark and Marielle.

By the end of their confessions, the girls had devoured all the pizza. Then they picked at the crusts and crunched the ice left in their cups.

"Do you remember that day we cut school and went up to the lake? Everything seemed so sure," Faith said.

"Yeah."

Faith leaned over the table. "It made me feel so good. I thought I knew how everything would turn out for the next hundred years or so. Didn't you feel that way, too?"

"Yes," KC admitted.

"I really did," Winnie said.

"But nothing is sure," Faith decided. "Since we've gotten here, everything's gone differently from how I expected. Sometimes I think that's terrible. But you know what?"

"What?"

"Other times I think that even though it's scary and makes me want to turn around and run back home, it's good."

Winnie and KC both reached out to touch Faith's arm.

"And I don't think I've figured out a whole lot yet, but I guess freshman year of college is supposed to be about change, right?"

Winnie and KC looked at Faith.

"At least you two are still here," Faith finally whispered.

"We are," Winnie reassured her.

KC agreed. "We're here. Like it or not, we're here."

They sat for a while, until the few other customers finished their pizzas and shuffled out. Soon the big-screen TV was dark, the lights were starting to dim, and Luigi was stacking chairs on top of the vacant tables.

The three of them stood up.

"Ready to go back to the dorms?" KC asked.

Winnie and Faith exchanged glances.

"Ready if you are," challenged Faith.

"How bad can it be?" responded Winnie. "Let's go."

They smiled at each other, linked arms, and strolled out onto University Avenue.

Twenty

“I found out that Dr. Hermann—you know, the prof we all have for Western Civ—is supposed to be a total killer.”

“Winnie, are you sure?”

“Three required papers, Faith,” insisted KC, confirming Winnie’s story. “That’s what I heard. Plus you have to read tons of literature from the period you’re studying.”

Winnie shook her head. “That’s what I get for signing up for a class just because you two are in it.”

It was late Sunday morning, and the girls were in Faith’s dorm room. While KC scribbled a post-card home, Faith typed out a resume to take over to the theater, and Winnie flipped through her Western Civ text.

"Hey, look at these Greeks in togas," Winnie said, holding up her book. "They should have lived in my dorm. I bet they knew how to party."

Faith and KC laughed.

"You know, Lauren's registered for this Western Civ class, too," Faith finally mentioned.

Silence.

"Well," babbled KC, filling in the pause. "Every other freshman takes Western Civ, so it's not so surprising that all four of us are in the same class."

Faith stared at her resume. KC stared at the door. Winnie stared blankly at her book.

"KC, don't keep looking at the door. Lauren will come back," Winnie insisted.

"Okay."

KC went back to her postcard, then threw down her pen and got up. "I couldn't believe it when the RA said Lauren went to stay with her mother at the hotel. I keep wondering if she's going to leave U of S. Maybe she already has. I talked to some other girls who rushed Tri Beta at breakfast this morning and nobody's seen her since the dance."

"What do you expect?" Winnie pointed out. "If I were her, I'd move back to Switzerland or Monaco, or wherever she's from."

"Winnie, that's not funny."

"I know, Faith. I'm just as worried as you are. I hope she comes back, too."

KC peered out through the leaves of the big oak tree. "You want to know the worst of it? The Tri Betas accepted her. She didn't even show up for the final interview, and she was still on the list of girls they invited to join."

"You're kidding," Winnie said.

"Why humiliate her and then ask her to join anyway?"

KC turned back. "Her mother."

They checked the door again, then went back to their projects. Faith finished her resume and stuck it in an envelope. KC addressed her postcard. Winnie put her book aside and looked through the course catalog.

"Hey, Win," said Faith. "Have you seen Josh?"

Winnie flipped pages and took a moment to answer. "It's pretty hard to avoid him. I passed him in the hall first thing this morning. He said hi and I said hi, and it was all very friendly and totally weird. It was kind of like we both wanted to talk about how weird it was, and neither of us knew what to say, so we didn't say anything."

Faith let out a little groan.

"I can handle it. I'll be so busy once classes start, I won't even think about him." Winnie looked back down at her catalog. "Hey maybe I should major in Volcanology."

"What's that? The study of *Star Trek*?"

"I hope not, KC. I've had enough of Captain Kirk for a while."

"What?"

"Forget it. Never mind," Winnie said, remembering the guy from the toga party.

"It's the study of volcanos," Faith volunteered.

Winnie sighed. "No comments about my explosive personality."

"Or your hot clothes," KC joked. "Mount St. Winnie."

"Lava lady," Faith said.

They all tried to laugh and kept staring at the dorm room door.

The last event of freshman orientation week was touch football out on the green. But by the third quarter, a storm was in full force. Pouring rain made going out for a pass a combination between mud wrestling and water skiing on grass. KC hadn't shown up, and Winnie was organizing her room with Melissa, but Faith was there. In spite of the rain, she was playing as hard as she could.

Brooks was leading one of the teams. Even through the wet and the mud, she could see the hurt and anger in his eyes. It was tolerable until they faced each other in a formation. Fist to the ground in a crouch, Faith and Brooks were nearly nose to muddy nose.

This was the first time Faith had really been able to see him up close since the breakup two nights before. She'd tried to call three times and had left messages with Barney, but Brooks hadn't called her back. And she knew he wouldn't any time soon.

"Twelve. Four thousand and eight. One-third and two-sixteenths, *Hike!*" Brooks called off in a voice that was supposed to sound carefree. He was wearing a joyless smile and making a point of being extra-friendly to his teammates—especially Dawn, the rock-climbing girl who lived in his dorm. And yet Faith could tell that the whole thing was an act for her benefit.

Look at me! she wanted to tell him. *I think I did the right thing, and I hope soon you'll think so, too.*

But Brooks wouldn't even get near her, so she couldn't say a thing. She waited until the end of the play and then left the game, heading away from the green. She liked the feel of the pelting water and hoped it would wash all confusion from her brain.

Finally, she took refuge under a bus stop shelter. The rain made a racket on the roof, and Faith was glad to be surrounded by so much noise. It made it easier to listen to the voices inside her head.

She'd taken a chance.

She'd made a change.

And she had to live with the consequences.

Faith threw back her head and screamed, as loudly as she could.

"Ahhhhhhhhh! Aghhhhhhhhhhhh!"

Her throat burned, but she was feeling better. That is, she was until she noticed the blurry shape of a young man standing just inside the shelter, staring at her.

"Excuse me," he hollered, over the sound of the rain. *"I'm looking for Faith Crowley. It's hard to tell who's who under all that mud. Do you know her? Could you give her a message?"*

He held a tan raincoat over his head, but was wet nonetheless. Rain streamed down his auburn hair and across his square jaw.

It was Christopher.

Faith began to shiver.

He was barely looking at her, and Faith knew he didn't recognize her. She thought of pretending to be someone else, and was only too aware that she probably looked like some insane person who'd wandered onto campus by mistake. But she was too tired, too wet, and too grungy to worry about it.

"I'm Faith," she admitted simply.

He squinted at her, then smiled. "You are,

aren't you? I've been looking for you," he said, "I just dropped by the theater and found your resume. I wanted to ask if you'd work on my show as assistant director. You'll get three credits for it. We start tomorrow. Every night from seven to ten, so it shouldn't interfere with classes."

Faith was amazed at her reaction. This was everything she'd wanted, but had been too chicken to go after. Strangely, it felt as if it were happening to someone else.

Christopher rubbed his hands together. "You cold?"

Faith shook her head.

"You're shivering."

"I know."

He cocked his head and tried to get an angle on her. "I'd really like it if you'd say yes."

Something still held Faith back. "You know Lauren Turnbell-Smythe, your dream date?" she blurted. "She's my roommate."

"Oh." Christopher looked away and frowned. A little trickle of rain was running down the side of his head and into his collar. "I did what I could. It wasn't my fault."

"Still, you didn't have to let it happen. You didn't have to carry on a cruel tradition like that. She still hasn't come back to the dorms. We don't know if she ever will."

"I'm sorry." Christopher stared out across the green. Then he faced her. "I knew Merideth was right when he suggested you."

"What does that mean?"

"Just that I like people who stand up for what they think. And who aren't afraid to say what they mean."

Faith said nothing.

Christopher leaned toward her, and for a moment everything stopped: the rain, the shivering. Christopher had taken out a handkerchief and was slowly wiping the mud from her face. Faith felt an electric surge of confidence and warmth.

"Thanks," she whispered.

He folded a clean corner of the handkerchief and dabbed her chin and her lips. Faith didn't take her eyes off his. The warmth was turning more powerful. Christopher's offer unleashed something bold inside her. And she didn't fool herself into thinking it was *only* an attraction to Christopher. That was part of it, but it was also an exciting realization that she had opened a door in her life. She had been brave enough to allow new people and challenges to come in.

Christopher stared at her a few seconds longer, then stood up quickly. "So are you interested in working on my play?"

"I love the theater."

"Then I'll see you tomorrow?"

Faith smiled. "Okay. You will definitely see me tomorrow."

"And you'll be my assistant?"

"I'll be the best assistant director in the world," she heard herself boast.

He smiled down at her, and for a moment neither moved. Christopher looked at her, his eyes taking in every inch of her face with appreciation and respect. Then, as quickly as he'd appeared, he put his coat over his head and jogged off.

"Okay!" Faith repeated, collapsing back on the bench. *"Okay!"*

She leaped up. No longer confused, she felt as if she could run hurdles or fly back to her dorm. She was charging on a blast of excitement so heady that she almost missed Winnie and KC, who were jogging in the opposite direction along the footpath outside the dining commons.

KC had a newspaper over her head, while Winnie wore a bright-red slicker. As soon as they saw Faith, Winnie twirled with her arms extended and KC dropped the paper to let the rain run down her face.

"We came to look for you," Winnie cried, running over and grabbing Faith around the waist.

"I couldn't stay inside, either," KC blurted, grabbing Faith, too. "We realized that it's all starting tomorrow. No matter what happened this week, tomorrow we'll start all over again."

"I know!" Faith yelled as thunder cracked and the rain came down even harder. "Tomorrow we start! Everything we've waited for since graduation. It all starts tomorrow!"

"Tomorrow!"

"Tomorrow!"

Faith hugged both of them. They laughed and frolicked in the rain, because they knew that come the morning, the real business of college would begin.

Here's a sneak preview of* Freshman Lies, *the second book in the compelling story of FRESHMAN DORM.

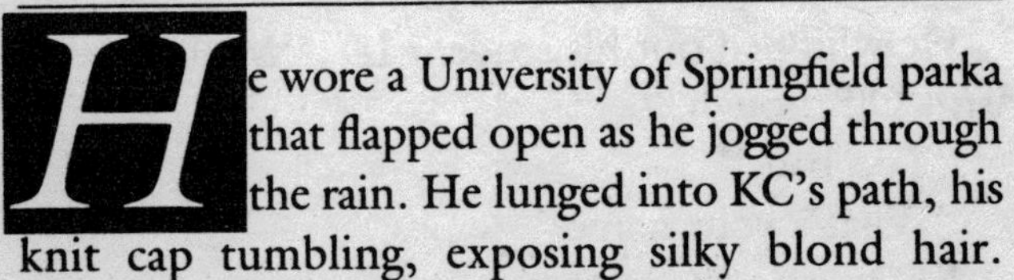

He wore a University of Springfield parka that flapped open as he jogged through the rain. He lunged into KC's path, his knit cap tumbling, exposing silky blond hair. Catching the hat as if it were a hard line drive, he looked to KC for appreciation.

"Don't I know you from somewhere?" he asked.

KC had never seen the guy before.

They were heading past the dorm dining commons, which smelled warm and salty. He carried an umbrella and a University bookstore bag.

KC stared straight ahead and kept on walking.

"Do I know you from Denver?"

"No."

"Summer camp?"

"I doubt it."

"Reform school?"

"Very funny."

"I wouldn't forget a girl who looks like you." He leered. "Where are you going?"

"To meet my girlfriends," she snapped. "Buzz off."

He hurried to keep up with her. "What a coincidence. My name is Buzz."

"Buzz?" KC gave him an icy smile. "Is that a name?"

He whipped out his student ID. "My last name isn't Off though."

"Too bad."

"What's your name?"

KC wasn't about to admit that her hippie parents had named her Kahia Cayanne.

"Okay, don't tell me. What dorm are you in?"

She didn't tell him she lived alone in an all-girls study dorm either.

"What's your major?"

KC strode faster.

"Okay, don't tell me. I met you last week, during freshman orientation. I'm sure of it."

"I don't think so."

"The toga party?"

"I didn't go."

He looked her up and down, taking in her long dark curls, her grey eyes, her briefcase, blazer and knife pleated skirt. "Oh. I get it. Sorority type. You were rushing with the geeks."

KC flinched. "The Greeks."

"That's what I said. The geeks."

"Ha ha."

"So what sorority house did you get into? And more important, do you still date poor, lonely dorm dudes who think you're gorgeous?" He put a hand to his heart and pretended to grovel.

KC glared.

"Are you reserved for frat brats?"

"I'm not reserved for anyone."

"So what house did you get into?"

KC's rage began to swell.

"Come on."

"Leave me alone!"

"You can tell me. Come on. Which house?"

Suddenly KC spun around and yelled in Buzz's face. "For your information, I'm not in any sorority. I'm a business major and I've never been to Denver, and I'm not interested in dating anybody!!! SO BUZZ OFF, BUZZ!"

"Hey, hey. Okay." Buzz backed away. "I just asked. You can't blame a guy for trying." He finally faded back and let her go.

"Guys," KC grumbled, breaking into a run and heading for Faith's dorm.

All KC needed was some guy hassling her about sororities and rush. Guys had caused plenty of trouble last week for her old friends, Faith and Winnie. One had also caused horrible trouble for Faith's roommate Lauren. And the last thing KC needed was some guy causing trouble for her.

When KC reached the parking lot, she saw Winnie and Faith admiring Lauren's new car. KC tried not to stare at the sparkling white BMW.

"It's really nice of you to take us all to dinner," Faith told Lauren as she and Winnie climbed in the back seat. "Where are we going?"

Lauren fiddled with her keys. "I thought I'd take you to The Blue Whale. If that's okay."

The Blue Whale was the most expensive restaurant on the exclusive Springfield Strand.

"KC," Lauren said in her breathy, refined voice.

KC froze. Finally she met Lauren's eyes. She wondered if Lauren were going to accuse her of betrayal or berate her for setting her up.

But instead Lauren said, "I heard about what you did, how you dumped those drinks on Marielle. Thanks."

"It was the least I could do," KC mumbled. "I'm sorry about what happened."

There was nothing else to say. KC reached for the car door.

Lauren held up her keys. A needy sweetness filled her round, pale face. "KC, do you want to drive?"

KC wanted to ignore Lauren's offer, but she couldn't help reaching for the keys. She changed places with Lauren and slid behind the wheel.

Not looking at Lauren, KC started the car with a little too much anger. The engine roared and the clutch jerked. When KC pulled out of the parking space, they skidded a little.

"Be careful," Faith warned.

"Whoa!" giggled Winnie.

KC was still so preoccupied over the injustice of the Tri Betas and Lauren treating them to such an expensive dinner that she didn't see the other car. It sped into the dorm parking lot, lights gleaming off slick pavement, screeching, skidding right for them.

"KC!" Faith screamed. "There's a car coming right at you!"

"HEY," Winnie yelled, "LOOK OUT!"

KC's pulse went wild. For a moment she wasn't sure what was happening. The other car was a blur of shiny dark. KC shoved her foot down on the brakes and the BMW slid. There was the wet squeal of rubber against asphalt. Water flew from beneath the wheels.

"STOP!" screeched Winnie.

Before KC could respond, the other car backed up, skidding and squealing again, until the driver's window was even with KC's. It was a vintage Corvette, perfectly restored and painted a lustrous black. The driver stuck out his head. He looked about eighteen or nineteen, slender with a tan, muscular arm. He suddenly fixed his eyes on KC.

"WHAT'S YOUR PROBLEM?" KC yelled as if all her frustration could come out in one big scream.

"No problem," he came right back, coolly, with a wry smile.

His coolness made KC even hotter. "You're not the only person who has to drive in this parking lot!"

"I'm not?" He stuck half his torso out to look. His long, straight hair reflected the overhead light.

In her panic, KC let the clutch pop out. The engine died. She desperately tried to restart the car.

"Need a driving lesson?" he mocked.

"No thanks," she spat back. "I'd prefer to stay alive."

"I'd prefer that too." He laughed.

KC felt like jumping out of the car for a fist fight. But instead she concentrated on restarting Lauren's car. "And I'd prefer never to run into you again."

He gunned his engine more loudly and laughed once more. "Oh, you'll run into me again. Don't you worry about that." Then the Corvette spun back around and sped off.

KC rested her face on the steering wheel. Her heart was pounding and she could barely catch her breath. "Sorry." She tried to calm herself. "Is everybody okay?"

Lauren reached over to reassure her.

KC pulled away. "I didn't see him. Do you still want me to drive?"

"Of course," said Lauren. "I don't mind."

"Guys," KC grumbled, forcing the BMW in gear again. "He can take his fancy car and drive off the end of the earth, for all I care. People like that make me nuts. Just because they have some fancy car, they think they own the world."